Country Lawyer
and Other Stories for the Screen

FAULKNER

A Comprehensive Guide to the Brodsky Collection

Country Lawyer
and Other Stories for the Screen

by
WILLIAM FAULKNER

Edited by
Louis Daniel Brodsky
and
Robert W. Hamblin

UNIVERSITY PRESS OF MISSISSIPPI
JACKSON/LONDON

CENTER FOR THE STUDY OF SOUTHERN CULTURE SERIES

The paper in this book meets the guidelines for permanence and durability of the Committee on Production Guidelines for Book Longevity of the Council on Library Resources.

Library of Congress Cataloging-in-Publication Data

Faulkner, William, 1897–1962.
    Country lawyer and other stories for the screen.

    "Published as a supplement to Faulkner, a comprehensive guide to the Brodsky Collection"—P.
    Contents: Country lawyer—The life and death of a bomber—The damned don't cry.
    I. Brodsky, Louis Daniel. II. Hamblin, Robert W.
III. Faulkner, a comprehensive guide to the Brodsky Collection. IV. Title.
PS3511.A86A6   1987   813'.52   86-21201
ISBN 0-87805-308-5 (alk. paper)

British Library Cataloguing in Publication
data is available.

Portions of this book have appeared in SOUTHERN MAGAZINE.

Contents

Preface

THIS VOLUME PUBLISHES for the first time three story outlines that William Faulkner wrote for Warner Bros. Pictures in the early 1940s.

Of the three narratives, by far the most interesting and impressive, to both general readers and Faulkner scholars, is "Country Lawyer." Attempts to develop a movie script based on Bellamy Partridge's book of reminiscences had been initiated in 1941; and Faulkner, who was assigned to the project from March 20 to April 6, 1943, was the sixth writer to be asked to try his hand at producing a workable script. Unlike the previous scenarists, however, Faulkner showed little inclination to remain faithful to Partridge's text. On the contrary, he transferred the setting from Phelps, New York, to his own fictional domain of Jefferson, Mississippi, and drew heavily upon this imaginary realm in creating an original story line. Thus "Country Lawyer" represents one of the few instances in which Faulkner sought to adapt and extend his Yoknapatawpha material to the purposes of Hollywood.

Readers versed in Faulkner's fiction and biography will find themselves traveling over familiar territory in "Country Lawyer." The tracing of the histories of the Galloway and Hoyt families through four generations and two wars is much like Faulkner's handling of the Sartorises, Compsons, Sutpens, McCaslins, and

Snopeses in the major fiction. The close relationship that exists between Sam Galloway, Jr., and his black companion, Spoot Moxey, parallels the interracial friendships in *The Unvanquished, Go Down, Moses,* and *Intruder in the Dust.* Rachel, Spoot's grandmother, is a reincarnation of Dilsey from *The Sound and the Fury* and (as Faulkner makes clear in his reference to the funeral oration and the nighttime shopping for ice cream) is similarly based on the actual Caroline Barr. The suddenness with which Sam Galloway falls in love with Edith Bellamy recalls the romantic situations in several Faulkner novels, including *Light in August* and *The Wild Palms,* as well as the family story that came down to Faulkner regarding the first meeting of his great-grandfather, W. C. Falkner, and Lizzie Vance. The comical description of the pig in the church belongs to the Southwestern yarnspinning tradition that Faulkner employs in "Mule in the Yard" and other stories. Linking the Galloway-Hoyt feud with *Romeo and Juliet* imitates Faulkner's frequent use, as in *Absalom, Absalom!* and *The Hamlet,* of mythical and literary archetypes. Such Yoknapatawpha names as "Tobe" ("A Rose for Emily"), "Mitchell" *(Sartoris),* "Coldfield"*(Absalom, Absalom!),* and "Spoot" ("Pantaloon in Black") are repeated in "Country Lawyer," and the inscription on the tombstone of Edith Bellamy Galloway is remarkably similar to the one on the monument erected for Eula Varner Snopes in *The Town.*

"The Life and Death of a Bomber" belongs to the considerable body of patriotic writing that Faulkner produced in support of the Allied effort in World War II. Other works in this category include the unproduced screenplays, "The De Gaulle Story" and "Battle Cry," and short stories such as "The Tall Men," "Two Soldiers," and "Shall Not Perish." "The Life and Death of a Bomber," written in January 1943 after a tour of an aircraft factory in San Diego, was initially planned to provide favorable publicity for Consolidated Aircraft the way an earlier Warner Bros. film, *Wings for the Eagle*, had done for Lockheed. By dramatizing how selfish interests contribute to a delay in the construction of a bomber and thus undermine national security, Faulkner's story makes a poignant argument for civilian support of the nation's servicemen. As Faulkner's letters from this period reveal, the opportunity to write wartime propaganda of this type provided an alternate means of serving his country after he had been judged too old for active duty as a pilot.

"The Damned Don't Cry" is one of a half-dozen story treatments that Faulkner completed in late 1941 and early 1942 in an attempt to secure a contract from a Hollywood studio. Mailed from Oxford to Warner Bros. in November or December 1941, this narrative represents a reworking of a previously-rejected screenplay based on Harry C. Hervey's novel, *The Damned Don't Cry*, published in 1939. Here, too, as in the case of "Country Lawyer," Faulkner has taken great liberties with the original plot, particularly in the handling of the central character, Zelda O'Brien. For Hervey's character who is victimized by circumstance, Faulkner substituted a strong-willed (and pragmatic) woman who exhibits remarkable resiliency and endurance in the face of a succession of tragic disappointments. Because of this psychological toughness (as well as her association with a

brothel), one may view Zelda as a precursor of the
Temple Drake who appears in *Requiem for a Nun.*

Perhaps the most significant aspect of the three works
printed in this volume is the insight they provide into
the working of Faulkner's creative genius. Faulkner ob-
served on numerous occasions that a work of fiction
derives from "observation, experience, and imagination." In their amalgam of incidents and ideas drawn
from first-hand observation, personal experience, reading, research, and imaginative invention, these stories
present capsule versions of Faulkner's fictive design.
Moreover, since these narratives represent initial stages
of the composition process, the reader is privileged to
view that process in an arrested state, frozen in place at a
critical early point. One advantage of such a perspective
is to be reminded of the primacy of traditional plot for
Faulkner. In these stories, presented as they are without
the overlay of multiple viewpoint, disrupted chronology,
and counterpointing of incident and mood, the plotting
of the action stands out in bold relief. Various critics
have noted that Faulkner's insistence upon a substantial
plot, upon story as story, sets him apart from most other
stream-of-consciousness practitioners. The contents of
this book serve to underscore the rightness of that judg-
ment—and, further, to suggest that plot not only is
crucial to Faulkner's technique but also well may have
been the component of any story upon which his rich
and versatile imagination initially seized.

The texts printed here are taken from the only known
copies of the three stories. Originally a part of the
Warner Bros. Story Department files, the materials are
now housed in Louis Daniel Brodsky's private Faulkner

collection, currently on deposit in Kent Library on the campus of Southeast Missouri State University, Cape Girardeau, Missouri. In editing the texts for publication, we have corrected obvious typographical and grammatical errors, regularized the spelling, punctuation, and capitalization, and adopted the standard paragraph indentation used in "Country Lawyer" rather than the block form employed in the other two works.

We are very grateful to Warner Bros., Inc., for granting permission to publish these stories, and we add our warm personal thanks to Marshall M. Silverman, the studio's executive in charge of legal affairs for theatrical feature films production. Mr. Silverman has graciously provided legal assistance and friendly encouragement not only for this project but also for our previous work with the Faulkner/Warner Bros. materials.

Robert W. Hamblin
Louis Daniel Brodsky

Country Lawyer

I

About 1890. Partridge comes to Jefferson, Mississippi, on foot. He has nothing but his law degree and a license to practice. He is just out of college. On his first day in town, he is on the front gallery of the hotel, with the usual town men who loaf there. A young man and a girl come up in a sulky, with a fine new horse. All the men are examining the horse, a mild sensation. The driver is boasting about it. The girl looks a little alarmed at the horse's spirit, etc.

The supper gong rings. The horse tries to bolt. Partridge and the other men finally catch and hold it, but in the excitement some damage is done to the hotel gallery. The sulky departs, while Partridge is still watching the frightened girl.

The proprietor of the hotel intends to sue the driver for the damage to the railing. The driver defies him. We learn that the driver is a wealthy young man, son of the town's banker. Partridge offers to take the proprietor's case. Partridge is a stranger, a foreigner. Nevertheless, the proprietor agrees to let Partridge handle the case, on a cut-rate price.

Partridge asks the proprietor who the girl is. The proprietor tells him she is the daughter of an old family, one of the first but decayed now, no money, etc., is supposed to be engaged to the driver. The proprietor intimates that who she is can never mean anything to

Partridge, asks Partridge why he wants to know. Partridge says calmly he intends to marry her.

The suit is brought before the local J.P. As everyone expected, the J.P. will not find for the newcomer. He finds for the defendant, with costs to the plaintiff. The proprietor grimly refuses to pay the costs. In the next shot, we see Partridge washing dishes in the hotel's kitchen to pay the costs of the case which, as its attorney, he lost. He does the work willingly and swiftly. He is not sullen about it; it must be done. The Negro cooks and waiters look down their noses at a white man doing Negro work. He is obviously "trash." But they actually sympathize with him; he has had a raw deal. But they feel that if he had any guts, he wouldn't let the proprietor treat him like this.

He realizes what he has undertaken to buck: the little town, all of whose people have known all the others for generations, who resent him not only because he is an outlander, but because he is what the Negroes first divined: a man without background of breeding, land, etc. But he will not give up and quit, because of the girl whom he has determined to marry.

The girl is aware of him, too. She was summoned as a witness in the abortive trial, reluctantly; a young lady had no business at such a place in the South at that time. She is attracted to him against her background and wish and all, out of sympathy for the underdog, and because he was forced to pay the costs of the case by doing "nigger" work, and because of his indomitable will to stay and take it. She is at the same time attracted by his youth and courage, repelled by the traditional belief in the insurmountable difference in their stations. That is, her upbringing tells her to be a snob; actually, she is not.

Everyone believes, the proprietor and a few others tell Partridge, that he will never get a start as a lawyer in that town, because he got off on the wrong foot, made the wrong people mad at him, etc. But he still refuses to give up. He will stay in the town just for the privilege of seeing the girl, hopelessly, now and then from a distance.

He knows horses, at least. He gets a job in the livery stable; he must live somehow. He drives the drummers and travelers in hired vehicles. He begins to drive a local lawyer, Hobson, on his country trips. Hobson becomes interested in him, but also advises him to go on. He tells Hobson why he will not, that he intends to marry Miss Bellamy. He is sorry of it, too. But his people fall in love just once; it has happened to him whether he wants it to or not, and there you are.

The rich young man, Hoyt, is engaged to Miss Bellamy. He senses a rival in Partridge, perhaps by instinct, presses for an early marriage. Miss Bellamy puts him off. Mrs. Bellamy perhaps knows why and perhaps Hoyt suspects. But Partridge doesn't know. He hasn't that much vanity, no confidence. He just knows the wedding is postponed and is glad.

As a proof to the town of his determination to stay and make the grade, Partridge now rents a small house, in which he lives alone, doing his own cooking, etc. Lawyer Hobson gives him a little legal work to do on the side: briefing cases, etc., privately.

Banker Hoyt's stable takes fire, burns, perhaps destroys valuable carriage horses. A middle-aged Negro, a local character, a tramp who sleeps around in people's barns, works only when he has to, without ambition, etc., is blamed for it. Hoyt in his rage has him arrested. Partridge begs Hobson to let him take the case. Hobson says he will only injure himself further, that the Negro won't mind staying in jail anyway, where he will be fed, and maybe he did do it, after all. Anyway, he should be broken of sleeping in people's stables, etc. But Partridge insists, believes the Negro is innocent. Hobson more or less washes his hands of the matter, but allows Partridge to use the facilities of his office, but on his own hook.

The Negro expects to be railroaded himself. He does not like Partridge's interference. The Negro has some of the snobbery of the white villagers. He had almost rather be sent to jail by what he calls "folks" than to be cleared by "trash." He tells Partridge to keep out of it: "You're gwinter git me in trouble sho enough. I been in jail befo'. Bein' in jail don't do nothin' but take up yo time for a mont' or two. Then they lets you out and first thing you know, you done forgot it."

But Partridge wins the case, frees the Negro, to everyone's surprise, including the Negro. But he has committed a worse lese majesty than ever now, is looked at cross-eyed by all the people whom he is hoping to establish himself with. But he was right; he has vindicated justice, saved the weak. But his thought is, "Now I've done it sure enough, I reckon." He is sober about it. He goes soberly home, cooks his lonely supper, eats it and goes to bed.

The next morning he is wakened by a noise in the kitchen. He goes there and finds the Negro, his wife and daughter, a young woman of about Partridge's age.

They are building a fire in the stove and getting ready to cook breakfast.

TOBE: *(Negro)* Good mawnin', Judge. Dis here's my wife and daughter.

PARTRIDGE: I didn't know you had a family.

TOBE: I been had one a good while. I jest ain't thought to mention um much.

Tobe explains they have come to work for him, in return for his winning the case. He says he can't afford servants, etc. Tobe says to never mind that; they don't want money right now, will wait on it, and they don't eat much. Partridge is alarmed; they have simply moved in. He refuses again; they must leave. He can't afford them. The Negroes are taken aback a little, pause.

Someone knocks on the door. Partridge thanks them, says they must go after breakfast and goes to the door. Waiting on the porch are five countrymen, in overalls, men like Partridge would have been if he hadn't turned lawyer, from the same background.

SPOKESMAN: You Judge Partridge?

Partridge tells them he is no judge, but they continue.

SPOKESMAN: We seen that case yesterday. If you can take a trifling barn-burning nigger and beat Colonel Hoyt with him, we figgered you would be a good man for us.

They have a case for him. Now he sees the future opening at last before him. At last he has got his foot in the door.

II

Some time has elapsed, perhaps a year. Partridge now has enough law practice to live on. It is still mostly with the country people who are of his own kind, who have quickly recognized his value to them, because of his honesty and the fact that he is not a blue-stocking aristocrat, and among Negroes, to whom he has become a champion, seeing that they receive justice even when he will get no pay from them. He has now given up trying to stop them from calling him "Judge."

He still has his little house, and his servants. He doesn't know himself exactly how it came about; the steps were so gradual. But now he has a servants' cottage in his back yard, in which Tobe and his wife Rachel and their daughter Caroline live. Rachel cooks for him; his clothes are taken care of. For a while he could not pay them wages, though he is doing better now.

For a little while Tobe seemed to have reformed, stayed at home, did a little work about the house. But now he has returned to his former tramp's life, sleeping wherever dark finds him, trifling and worthless. But Rachel is a different sort, and the daughter will also be a good woman. Her mother is training her to be so. We see here a relationship established upon mutual respect between the white man and the two Negro women which will endure.

(NOTE: Since we are changing this story, taking liberties with it, perhaps we will change this man's name. With his background, he will have a name out of North Ireland or the Scottish Lowlands, perhaps Galloway, Samuel Galloway. I'll call him that from now on.)

Sam's position in the town has improved. He is not
ignored by the blue bloods. To them, he simply does not
exist socially, any more than the dry-goods clerk or the
barber. But his honesty and reliability and his soundness in law have established him in the respect and
consideration not only of his clients but of the other
men, business men, of the town. He has even found a
social niche, among people like himself who are new-
comers there, who have moved in from the country or
from other parts. He belongs to a church. Not Pres-
byterian or Episcopal, where the old families go, but to a
Methodist or Baptist church, new people, not rich.

He makes no effort to see Edith Bellamy. His attitude
now is almost fatalistic. He saw her, he fell in love with
her, he knows it is forever, yet he has no reason to hope.
He will simply stay in Jefferson, where she is; he would
prefer to be in the same town and not have her than to
be anywhere else and not have her. He knows she is
engaged to the rich young Hoyt, with whom he can
compete only if he could get Hoyt into a law court.
When Hoyt and Edith marry, which he believes they will
do some day, then will be time for him to move on.

He does not even know that he has got himself into
her mind and thoughts. She may have striven against it,
but he is there, because of the qualities of honesty,
dependability, gentleness, which his poor white and
Negro clients have seen and which the men of the town
have seen, divined. Actually, she was ripe for love, and
Sam had the qualities necessary to arouse it in her. Some
female instinct might have seen in Sam's peasant blood
that strength which was exhausted in her own blood. We
will simply show that she thinks of him, does not want

to, has given her pledge to another man, knows her
mother and family will be horrified at an attachment to
this unknown plebeian. Perhaps she feels herself that
loving him will be lese majesty: a betrayal of her tradition, etc.

FADE IN

A montage of court scenes, first in the countrified
J.P.'s court, then in the Circuit Court, as Sam's clients
change and improve in quality as he becomes not only a
crusader but a better and more skillful lawyer. He takes
cases, regardless of who the plaintiff is, color or condition, only when he believes he is serving justice, protecting the weak. Sometimes he loses. His client may not
be able to pay costs, fine, etc. Sam pays them, to keep the
client, Negro or white, out of jail.

(We will be careful not to make him a tin god nor a
sap, either. He wants to earn his honest penny, too. His
only hope of ever getting Edith is to be able to support
her, give her an establishment as near as possible to what
she will have relinquished—if she ever would accept
him, which he still dares not put to the test, and at this
point has no actual hope of putting it to the test. He
believes that if you are just, honest, and industrious, the
world, mankind, will not let you starve. We want to show
a man who believes in the innate soundness of mankind,
people, and in the simple verities of honor, dignity,
justice, courage, etc.)

He has done so well, made so many friends among
the lesser people of the county, has established a name
for honesty and reliability and consideration for the

weak, that he is approached by a delegation of smaller men, little merchants, farmers, etc., who ask him to run for the state legislature. He refuses, explains that he will have no chance to win, does not want the office, thanks them. They are disappointed, and retire.

Later, to his surprise, he is approached by a man who has a lot of political weight, who could get him elected if he wished. The man makes him the same offer. Sam knows he can have the office now, simply for entering the race. He wonders why, begins to smell a rat. He learns what is up. There is a lobby going on in the legislature which will work an injury to some of the small farmers of the county. Perhaps the condemnation of land for some financial purpose. Perhaps some of the older town people, such as Mrs. Bellamy, a widow and stupid, have their money invested in the scheme by the unscrupulous people running the lobby.

Sam realizes that the office is a bribe for his vote. When he refuses, the agent puts on pressure, tells him he will be ruined in the town as a lawyer if he does not. Finally Sam devolves a scheme by which, in running for the office and losing, he can defeat it, expose it. If he does this, he will very likely jeopardize and ruin his future. Nevertheless, he does so, makes the race, exposes and hamstrings the plan, is defeated.

Now he has a definite element in the town against him. He has been working at a case which would have meant his first sizeable fee, the first thing yet which would have given him any base to hope for Edith. At the same time, he hears that Edith and Hoyt's wedding has been set. He does not know that Mrs. Bellamy, in her anger at losing the profit, has brought the pressure on

Edith to set the date. All he knows is that the wedding, which he has feared all along and has hoped against, why he doesn't know, is announced.

He goes home that night, sad, discouraged, hopeless now. He tells Rachel he is going to leave Jefferson. She knows why. A woman, she has divined his feeling about Edith. But being a Negro, she can say nothing. She says, all right, they will move then.

SAM: Not you. I will have to start over again, you see— in a livery stable again. We'll have to say goodbye, too.

Rachel says all right, if that must be. She says she will begin to get his things together, for him to go on to the church supper he promised to attend, forget his troubles for the evening.

SAM: Drown them in ice cream, eh? Well, maybe my troubles were of so little weight to begin with that ice cream will drown them.

He leaves the house, to go to the church supper. It is a small sect, Campbellite Baptist perhaps, composed of little people like him, country-bred people, whose kin were the ones whose land he saved. They know it, are his friends, make him welcome.

The scene between Mrs. Bellamy and Edith has taken place. Under pressure, Edith has agreed to let the wedding take place tomorrow. The plans have been in existence for a long time, everybody is expecting it. Mrs. Bellamy can send the word out and the wedding can be tomorrow. She rushes Edith into it, takes advantage of Edith's distracted state, since Edith now knows what Sam has done, as the whole town does.

Edith agrees, under one condition: that her mother

permit her to be free for this last night. Mrs. Bellamy may know what is in Edith's mind, but since Edith has passed her word, and to bring the matter off, Mrs. Bellamy agrees to let Edith be free for this evening. (Edith has agreed to the marriage mainly because her mother has told her that Sam is going to leave Jefferson. If she thinks at all at this time, she thinks she is going to tell Sam goodbye—that sort of thing.)

Edith hurries alone (this is daring enough for a young girl of that place and time) to Sam's house. Rachel tells her where Sam is. Edith hurries on. Rachel knows what is up, too: that Edith is ready to take Sam, only neither she nor Sam actually know it.

Edith goes to the church supper. The people make her welcome, of course. But they are surprised to see her here. She does not belong to this sect, none of her people and kind do; most of them know her only by name, have never spoken to her save in passing on the street. They can see that she is in an upset state. She finds Sam; he is surprised, too. What takes place between them is actually a love scene, though neither one knows it. Edith, though she does not know it, is saying, "Take me." Sam doesn't get it because he has never for one second anticipated such as this. They are even a little stiff with one another. Edith has to explain her presence here. She says she understands what he has done to preserve the land, wants him to know she respects the act, etc.

> **SAM:** *(awkward, at a loss)* And you are to be congratulated, too, I understand. I mean—only you don't congratulate the bride, but the groom—

They both are embarrassed. The people are covertly watching them. Edith becomes aware of her boldness in coming, feels with despair that she and Sam are growing further and further apart, that the matter is hopeless. In the conversation, in her excitement and loss of poise, she babbles, talks rapidly. Sam learns that she promised to marry tomorrow only to get permission to come out tonight. She leaves, hurries away: Goodbye, goodbye, she will never see him again, etc.

Sam now believes this is the end. He goes home, sadly. Rachel is waiting up for him. He is surprised, but too troubled to pay much attention. She learns how Edith came to the supper, something about what happened. She wishes to tell him the woman is offering herself to him and that he is a blind fool without courage to do nothing about it. But she is a Negro and can't say much. But she has determined what she will do. Sam goes into his room; he will leave Jefferson tomorrow. He tells Rachel to see that the buggy is at the gate at noon.

The next morning Sam is packing up to leave Jefferson for good. Rachel goes to the Bellamy house. The wedding party is there: the bridesmaids, the sewing women getting the bride's dress ready, etc. Nobody pays any attention to Rachel, who is known to the Bellamy servants.

Rachel goes up to Edith's room, gets Edith alone, tells Edith Sam is sick, lets Edith get the idea that Sam has tried to kill himself. Edith must go to him. She is shocked, hysterical. Rachel helps her to pull herself together and get out of the house by the back and go to Sam's house by back streets, etc., not to be seen in this state.

Edith runs into the room where Sam is packing. She finds he is not hurt, but is merely going away. But the thing happens on which Rachel had counted. Edith runs to Sam, clings to him.

EDITH: Take me with you!

After Sam quiets her, he reminds her that she gave her word to her mother last night; in honor and decency they must go to Mrs. Bellamy and retract the promise. Edith is afraid to, wants to leave now, but Sam insists. Nothing else will be right to her mother. Edith knows what will happen, wishes to shield Sam from it, begs him to let her go alone. Sam refuses; he owes that himself to his wife's mother.

They go to the Bellamy house. The bridesmaids are there, dressed. Everyone is hunting high and low for Edith when they walk in. Edith tells Mrs. Bellamy she is going to marry Sam. A violent scene takes place, in which Mrs. Bellamy vents her fury on Sam, the parvenu, the climber, repudiates her daughter, never to see her again.

Sam helps Edith from the house. She says, let's go, hurry, get away from here. Sam tells her gently that the business is not finished. There remains her fiancé yet. Edith can't face that at all. Sam does not intend for her to; that is his job. So he leaves Edith waiting in the buggy with Rachel and he goes to the Hoyt home, where the father and son are ready to leave for the wedding.

They have already been warned of what has happened. When Sam returns Hoyt's ring, Hoyt snatches up a riding whip and strikes Sam across the face. Sam does not retaliate. Hoyt begins to taunt him with cowardice when the elder Hoyt intervenes, stops his son, tells the son that he has hit a man who at the moment can't resist.

HOYT, JUNIOR: *(raging)* Then he will never resist because he'd better never show his face in this town again.

Hoyt, Junior, rushes out.

HOYT, SENIOR: *(to Sam)* You have taken his wife. Now you have taken his blow. Better call it even and go. My advice to you, too, is not to come back here. Good day.

Sam returns to the buggy, where Edith waits in terror and dread. She sees the welt on his face, knows what has happened, and why Sam had to take the blow. They tell Rachel goodbye, drive on.

Hoyt, Junior, goes to Mrs. Bellamy's. The wedding party is waiting, the bridesmaids curious, excited, interested: this is a Roman holiday indeed. Hoyt enters, looks about as the girls watch him. One of them is an old flame of his.

HOYT: I have come to a wedding. Who here can marry without having to ask a jackleg lawyer first? *(he looks about, chooses the old sweetheart)* You.

She accepts him, on the dare. They are married that day.

Sam and Edith in the buggy, eloping. Edith is quieter now. Sam says something to her. She answers, calling him "Mr. Galloway."

SAM: Mr. Galloway? Can't you say Sam even yet?

She is shy, hides her face against him, mumbles something.

SAM: What? What did you say?

He tries to raise her face, but she still hides it.

EDITH: I'll have to get used to it.

He embraces her with one arm, drives on.

FADE OUT.

III

Sam does not leave Jefferson. He returns after his honeymoon and starts again to practice law. He has won the girl he loves; he feels the strength to dare and conquer anything now. The Hoyts and the town cannot beat him.

He had expected to face all sorts of difficulties when he returned to Jefferson, not only from the power and hatred of the Hoyts, but from their friends and members of the other older families who would resent a pedigreeless upstart marrying one of their daughters.

But he found very little of this, or at least he realized quickly that what he did meet was not important. He still had his old friends and clients, and new ones came to him, not only because of his reputation as a lawyer and an honest man, but because he had defied the snobbish convention of the town's caste system for love, and had been successful. So all that remained of any size was the hatred of Carter Hoyt for him. Sam realized quickly that this would never cease. He speaks to Edith about this, offers to leave Jefferson if she wishes. She refuses. His life is here; he has worked too hard to get a start.

Carter Hoyt and his wife now have a child, a daughter. Sam and Edith have a daughter and a son. The children know of the enmity between the two families; they themselves take up the feud in their childish way. Rachel's daughter, Caroline, is married also and has a son, a little older than Sam's. Sam's son is named Samuel Bellamy Galloway. The Negro child was named by Rachel, Sam Galloway Moxey. Rachel is now getting pretty old.

When James was born, his mother died. Rachel and Caroline have raised the two white children. Caroline fed the white baby at her breast along with her own. Thus they ate and slept together as infants and have continued to do so, while old Rachel trained them in conduct, taught them manners, cleanliness, etc., severe and strict and yet fond, too. Rachel does this not only out of humanity and maternal feeling for the motherless children, but because she knows she was responsible for Edith's marrying Sam, and so Rachel feels that in a sense it is her fault that the children have no mother, that Sam in his grief might have felt this, too, though he has never said so.

FADE IN

CLOSE SHOT of Edith's monument over her grave in the cemetery:

EDITH BELLAMY GALLOWAY

1872   1894

wife of

SAMUEL WINDMAN GALLOWAY

"Her husband praiseth her
Her children rise and call her blessed"

It is about 1905. It is a Sunday afternoon. The carriage, Tobe driving, waits in the background. Sam stands beside the grave while his daughter, Edith, kneels, putting flowers in a vase on the grave. Edith is about twelve. Edith finishes the flowers, rises. She and her father return to the carriage. Sam stops.

SAM: *(to Tobe)* Where are the boys?

TOBE: *(calls out of scene)* Sam! Yawl come on here!

CLOSE SHOT of the white boy and the Negro boy in a hedge, climbing after a bird's nest. They return to the carriage, where Sam and Edith are now in the back seat.

WHITE BOY: *(to Tobe)* It won't take but a minute. We almost had it.

TOBE: Nemmine that. You git in here. We going home.

The boys get in the front seat with Tobe.

WHITE BOY: Gimme the reins. I'll drive.

He takes the reins; the carriage goes on. As the carriage passes along the street, Sam sees a Negro man. The Negro is a client who was accused of stealing a pig and whose case Sam won. Sam stops the carriage, calls the Negro, who approaches.

SAM: Next time you steal any hogs, I want one of them.

NEGRO: *(guffaws)* Lawd, Judge, you sho is comical.

The carriage goes on home.

There is a rainstorm that night, thunder and lightning. Rachel is sending the two boys to bed in their room. The white boy sleeps in the bed, the Negro sleeps on a pallet bed on the floor. They are in their night-shirts, romping and scuffling, making so much noise that Rachel comes in and orders them into bed, firm, a little irascible. She takes no nonsense from them when she commands them to anything. They quiet. The white boy gets into the bed; the Negro takes the pallet. Rachel says goodnight, tells them to be quiet, puts out the lamp and leaves. The lightning glares, thunder rolls. The white boy rises on his elbow, looks down at the Negro.

WHITE BOY: Come up here with me.

NEGRO BOY: And have Mammy come in here and whup the tar outen both of us? Naw.

WHITE BOY: Then I'm coming down there.

NEGRO: All right. Come on. Then see if you can't shut up and lemme go to sleep.

The white boy gets onto the pallet with the Negro.

One morning when the house wakes, there is a strange pig in the back yard. They know at once where it came from, though the pig-stealing client denies it.

The two boys adopt the pig at once. They purloin food from the kitchen for the pig, until Rachel stops them. Mr. Galloway buys feed for it; the two boys feed the pig so much that Mr. Galloway objects. Then the boys get jobs, cutting grass, etc., to buy extra food for the pig. Soon it becomes a complete pet, will follow them around like a dog, until at last winter comes and the pig is ready to kill.

By this time, the pig is such a pet of the whole family that nobody could bear to eat it. Mr. Galloway does not like the idea of continuing to buy feed for a pet hog, but he lets the matter slide, knowing how it would break the boys' hearts.

One Sunday the pig gets out, follows the family to church, enters the church. A scene follows, in which the congregation and the two boys try to catch the pig, which darts among the pews, until the whole church is in an uproar. At last the pig is captured.

The boys take the pig home. They are terrified. They saw Mr. Galloway's displeasure. Now he will insist that the pig be made into pork. Something must be done, and at once. So they kidnap the pig, sneak it out the back. They have quite a time finding some safe place to leave it. The pig itself doesn't seem to realize what it faces and it will not cooperate. It escapes. In the chase, the white boy falls and gashes his arm so that a scar will be left. They catch the pig, bind the hurt arm, and go on. They are gone all that night.

Sam and Rachel and Caroline are frantic with worry, Sam and Rachel grimly angry, too. They find the boys the next day, bring them home. Sam is good and mad now. He makes Rachel leave the room while he interrogates the two boys.

The boys see his anger, are terrified. To protect themselves in their desperate strait, the white boy says that the pig escaped and they were simply following it. Sam knows he is lying. Sam asks the Negro boy. The Negro boy backs up his foster brother, supports the lie. Sam turns to his son.

SAM: You lied.

WHITE BOY: *(terrified, whispers)* I lied.

SAM: Go to the library.

The white boy goes out. Sam follows, ignoring the Negro boy. Rachel enters, stops him.

SAM: *(to Rachel)* He lied. I'm going to whip him. For the lie. I would have saved the pig, too, if I had been him. But he lied. Stand aside, Rachel.

RACHEL: Are you going to whip Spoot, too? He lied, too.

SAM: No. That's Caroline's business—or yours. Get out of the way.

RACHEL: If one of them's bad enough to need whipping, and good enough to be saved by it, then so is the other one.

She faces him down. He knows she has beaten him. She turns quietly to the two boys, who are watching her in fearful respect. The white boy knows she has saved him, as she has always done.

RACHEL: *(to Spoot)* Go get your paw's strop. Then both of you come to the kitchen.

They go out. She follows.

In the kitchen, she whips them both with the razor strop. Then she gets them a piece of cake each, gives it to them as they wipe the tears away.

RACHEL: Go out on the back steps and eat it. Don't you drop a crumb in this house.

FADE OUT.

IV

Time: about 1917. Sam is in his late forties. He has done well at law. Now he lives in a big old house, one of the fine ones in the town; probably it is the old Bellamy house which he has restored. He is still active at his practice, and he has not changed. He still champions the weak, tries to see justice done. When justice and the law conflict, everyone knows that Sam will twist the letter of the law to make it fit justice. He could have become a politician, been a Congressman or perhaps the Judge which people still call him, if he had wanted to.

Rachel is now quite old. Her duties are finished; she is simply the matriarch, whom the white children and the black ones, too, still hold in the same fear and respect. Caroline is about the same age as Sam. She has now become the Rachel of Sam's young manhood and marriage and the beginning of his family.

Edith is about twenty-two, married, has a son, Samuel Galloway Coldfield. Sam Bellamy, Sam's son, is twenty-one. He is in school at Yale, learning law. He still has the scar on his wrist from the pig episode.

Spoot, Caroline's son, Sam Galloway Moxey, the Negro, is twenty-one.

Margaret Hoyt, Carter Hoyt's daughter, is nineteen. She is at school in Virginia. The two families still do not speak.

FADE IN

1917. March. Spoot is being married. The wedding takes place in the Negro church. It is decorated; a pew has been held for Spoot's white people. Sam, Edith, old

Rachel, Tobe and Caroline are in the pew as the wedding takes place.

DISSOLVE TO:

A letter from Sam at Yale to his family. Perhaps he is writing it in his study; perhaps Sam or Edith is reading it to the others, Caroline present, Edith's fiancé, Emory Coldfield, perhaps Spoot and his wife.

"So Spoot's married at last. Well, well. He stole a march on me. But never mind. The Prom comes off next week. They always have a new batch of girls up then, and perhaps I can find one that you will approve of as the next Mrs. Sam Galloway. Not you and Edith: it's Mammy and Caroline she'll have to please. . . ."

DISSOLVE TO:

Voice on track over DISSOLVE.

VOICE: So it was Romeo and Juliet again, the old, old story of Capulet and Montague. . . .

At the Prom in New Haven. Sam, Junior, and Margaret Hoyt meet at the dance. Neither expected to see the other. They recognize each other at once, of course. Sam hesitates only a moment, then he walks up to Margaret and her escort, takes possession of her, tells the escort to excuse him; he and Margaret are old friends, before the escort has time to do anything about it.

MARGARET: *(resists)* No!

SAM: *(will not be denied)* This is not Jefferson. Come on. The chaperones are watching us. Let's dance.

Margaret has to dance with him. She has not had time to refuse and control the situation. So they fall in love, who as children grew up to think the other family were monsters, etc., who made faces at one another when they passed on the street. For a while Margaret, out of loyalty to her father, tries to fight against it, but in vain.

Before the evening is over, she has given up. It is as if they have both accepted what they cannot help, along with a foreknowledge of the tragedy which it will bring. They are not even talking any more. They just dance together. It has become a scandal almost. She has insulted her escort, ignored everyone else; the chaperones are all looking cross-eyed at her.

At last the dance ends. The chaperone in whose charge Margaret is, comes, coldly outraged and disapproving, and gathers Margaret up. Margaret seems to wake up. The chaperone is herding her away. With everyone still looking on, Margaret kisses Sam. Sam tries to cover up for her. (This is 1917, remember.)

SAM: It's all right. We are engaged.

The chaperone makes a tart rejoinder, takes Margaret away.

DISSOLVE TO:

A montage showing the Declaration of War, April 1917.

DISSOLVE TO:

Sam goes to Margaret's Virginia school to see her. The interview takes place in a small reception room, with a chaperone present. The chaperone sits some distance away and is knitting; nevertheless, she is there, and Sam and Margaret know they have no chance to be alone.

They are both sober, very grave now. Margaret is troubled over what she knows will be her father's reaction to this news. She has not told him yet, dreads the necessity of having to. But Sam intends to go to the war; no young man of spirit could do less. He will quit school, return after the war and become a lawyer if he has the chance. But now he must be a soldier. But he wants to be married first; he wants to know a little anyway of what he will be fighting for. Margaret will not marry him without telling her father. At last they agree that Margaret shall quit school, too, go home and ask her father's permission.

They return to Jefferson. Edith's fiancé is already a soldier, an officer in Quartermaster or some non-combatant corps, will very likely not be sent overseas. Their wedding day is set now, and now the wedding can be a double one.

When old Sam hears the news, he is shocked. He had not expected this from fate: that his only son should have chosen for his wife the daughter of the man whose blow he had had to take that day for the sake of his bride, the man who for twenty years had been his enemy, had tried to ruin him and drive him from the town. His first impulse is to refuse flatly to give his consent. But against this there is not only his love for his children, but all his principles of right and justice. At last he says he will make Margaret welcome as his son's wife, and let the old feud die.

But then young Sam hears from the frantic Margaret.

Her father is so bitter against the match that she is afraid. Hoyt has said he will not answer either way, will give an answer only on condition that old Sam go to him and request it.

Old Sam knows at once what this means. It means that Hoyt not only will probably refuse his consent in the end, but in the meantime he is going to force old Sam to eat crow, come and humble himself in vain before the man who has injured him. Old Sam is furious. He flatly refuses. He even goes further and retracts the consent to the marriage which he has already given; no Hoyt shall marry into his family, even if Hoyt himself would consent now.

Young Sam fires up, too. He is like his father. But he restrains himself where the older man has let go. He says that he and Margaret will need nobody's consent and that no man can stop them. Old Sam, in his bitter rage, says sure, Sam may not need anybody's consent; since the girl is a Hoyt, maybe he won't even need a wedding license—

SAM, JUNIOR: Father!

Old Sam hushes. He has gone too far. He did not mean that.

SAM, JUNIOR: You will take that back. Then you will apologize.

There is a commotion at the door. Old Rachel, old and feeble now, is trying to enter. Caroline is trying to restrain her. But Rachel enters anyway.

RACHEL: *(to Sam, Senior)* You take that back. You didn't mean that. Come on, now.

SAM, SENIOR: Yes. I didn't mean it. I'm sorry, Sam. Elope with her, then. I eloped with your mother—

SAM, JUNIOR: She won't. She gave her father her word. Hoyts keep their words, too, like you taught us, me and Spoot, not to lie.

RACHEL: *(to Sam, Senior)* You never stole Miss Edith, though. You went to her maw and told her. And you even went to the man she was already promised to and told him. You got Miss Edith. What you got to hate Carter Hoyt about?

SAM, SENIOR: *(quietly, knows he is beaten)* Yes. Yes.

So Sam, Senior, goes to Hoyt, to ask for the daughter. This is just what the furious, vindictive Hoyt, who has nursed the old hatred for twenty-five years, has been waiting for. He has a riding crop on the table, tells Sam he has wondered how long it would be before Sam would come back to get the other side of his face striped so they would balance.

Hoyt is a semi-invalid. Sam knows this. But it is not only this which restrains him. He knows he must get Hoyt's consent. But he soon realizes that Hoyt does not intend to give it, is merely taking revenge. Still old Sam restrains himself, while Hoyt demands one concession of his man's pride after another, until at last Hoyt becomes so outrageous that Sam cannot bear it any more and leaves.

He returns home. He is raging, furious. Sam, Junior, Edith, Rachel and Caroline are waiting for him. When he enters the room, he can hardly speak.

SAM, SENIOR: And, remember! It's not Carter Hoyt that forbids this marriage! I do! It's me! I forbid it!

SAM, JUNIOR: Then I won't ask for your consent.

SAM, SENIOR: You won't get it. If you marry that girl, you have ceased to be my son. You will not enter this house again.

Edith tries to stop him. Caroline and Rachel watch anxiously. But he and Sam, Junior, cannot be stopped now.

SAM, JUNIOR: *(starts out)* I'll send for my clothes tomorrow. Can I have that much time?

SAM, SENIOR: They will be packed and sitting on the front gallery this afternoon. *(to Edith and Caroline)* Go and pack Mr. Sam's clothes.

EDITH: Father!

SAM, SENIOR: *(thunders)* Did you hear me?

Old Rachel is now in an argument with Caroline, who is trying to make her leave the room.

RACHEL: Nemmine that. I'm gonter talk. I'm older than he is. I done seen more foolishness than even he can do. *(to Sam, Senior)* Mister Sam—

SAM, SENIOR: *(furious still)* You have already talked too much. It was you who went and said whatever it was to Miss Edith to bring her to me, whom I was to lose while I was still a young man capable and needing love, who was to bequeath to me a son who—son who—

He is about to break down but restrains himself. Caroline takes Rachel's arm and turns her.

CAROLINE: Come on, Mammy.

The two Negro women exit. Edith watches her father timidly, grieving.

EDITH: Father—

SAM, SENIOR: *(pulls himself together)* He'll be all right. Hoyt was packed up to leave when I was there. He and the girl are going to South America. Sam'll be back.

Sam goes to the Hoyt home. Perhaps they have already gone, or perhaps he has a last scene with the tearful Margaret in which he learns that this is all of it. He returns, gets his packed bags from his father's gallery, and leaves.

Inside the house, old Sam is convinced that young Sam will return when he finds his love is lost to him. He is merely waiting for Sam to come in and say, "Father, I was wrong. I'm sorry."

But Sam doesn't come. At last old Sam finds the bags are gone. Now, since he has proved his point, he is willing to meet his son more than halfway. He goes to the hotel. Sam, of course, will be there; old Sam himself will make the first step, say, "Come back home, son."

But Sam, Junior, is not there. Old Sam learns that he has left town on the afternoon train. Now old Sam is beaten. There is not only no erring son to apologize to him; there is no son for Sam himself to apologize to. Sam, Junior, has beaten him.

He returns home. His mood is adamant now. He will never make the first step now. He offered to and his son spurned him. Now the son must come to him. Rachel is there listening, saying nothing. Sam repeats: Never will he make the first step, never, never. Where young Sam goes, he neither knows nor cares. He is a thwarted and baffled man of fifty, trying to preserve his own dignity.

Edith and Caroline know this, that only he can change himself from inside. But by that time, nobody knows where Sam, Junior, will be. Caroline quietly leaves the room. Edith carries the scene on, tries to quieten her father, etc. Caroline is still there. Suddenly Spoot's wife enters, hurried and alarmed.

SPOOT'S WIFE: Mister Sam—Mama—

Sam and Caroline look at one another, react, exit hurriedly, Edith and the young Negress following. Rachel has had a stroke. She lies on the path like a light small bundle of sticks and rags as the others hurry in. Sam raises her and carries her to her cabin, which we will see completely now: the quilt Rachel made herself, the old lamps and ornaments which she has saved all her life; the pictures, religious mottoes, etc. They put her to bed and send for the doctor. She will recover.

When Sam wakes the next morning, the back yard is full of Negroes of all ages from infants to grandparents. Sam sends for Tobe, asks who the devil this is.

TOBE: They's just some mo' of mine and Rachel's family you spoke of that day. I jest ain't thought to mention these neither.

Rachel's cabin will not begin to hold them; her kitchen

will not begin to cook enough food. They stay for days. The women and children sleep on the floor in the cabin; the men and boys sleep on the gallery or on the ground. It is a holiday for them as they cook their food over open fires on the ground and eat it picnic fashion.

Rachel enjoys it, too, as she recovers. She is already the matriarch of a tribe; now she becomes a tyrant, making them fetch and carry for her all day long as she improves until she can sit on the porch among them. She tyrannizes over the white people, too, over Sam and Edith.

One night Sam has undressed, lies in his nightshirt, has been reading, is just about to turn out the light to sleep when the slow sound of feet approaches on the stairs and one of the strange Negro men enters.

SAM: *(with resignation)* All right. What this time?

NEGRO: She want strawberry, this time.

Sam gets up, asks the Negro to hand him his pants and shoes, draws the pants over his nightshirt, leaves the room. He gets his car, drives downtown to a drugstore, buys a quart of strawberry ice cream, returns, gives it to the waiting Negro, takes off his pants and shoes, gets into bed, relaxes, reaches for the light, sighs.

They have a letter from Sam, Junior. It is not angry, just quiet, matter-of-fact. He is in an officers' training camp. The day after the family read this letter, Spoot is missing. He has gone and enlisted, too.

Edith's wedding is held, with military pomp as she marries her quartermaster officer. Rachel, Caroline and Spoot's wife, clean and fresh and decorous, are in a back pew to watch Sam give away the bride.

Spoot's wife, Alice, has a letter from Spoot. Neither she nor Spoot can read or write. Caroline brings the letter to Sam. Spoot has got a soldier who can write to write it for him. The scribe can't write much either. The letter says:

"Der wife i getting along Fine I aint caught mister Sam yet they say we going over Sea soon maybe i find him yit your loving husband Corporal Sam Galloway Moxey number A.P.O. no 0518 A.E.F."

They receive a letter from Sam, short and quiet like the other. He tells them goodbye and gives his address: First Lieut. Sam B. Galloway, A.P.O. #0716, American Expeditionary Forces, France. (We can write a letter in here that will break your heart.)

FADE OUT.

V

Time: October, 1918. Edith is now married. She is going to have a child, is living with her father while her husband is away on duty at some camp in the States.

Alice, Spoot's wife, has a boy.

Old Rachel is more or less confined to her bed. Otherwise she is sound and rational enough.

Margaret Hoyt is married. The family have heard about it, though the Hoyts have not returned yet.

(A suggestion to change the line. Edith has been married several years. The child she now expects will be the son. She already has a daughter. I would like to play scenes in which old Rachel is training the little girl to be a decent woman. Rachel and she sit in Rachel's house

while the little girl learns to piece quilts, learns to cook,
sew, sweep, and to be always truthful.)

FADE IN

October, 1918. The weather is damp, wet, cold; the
sad end of the year. Old Sam, Edith, Caroline and
Spoot's wife and the children are in the library. They
have received a letter from Sam. Old Sam reads it aloud:

> "I was assigned to this company because I was a South-
> erner, and therefore I knew Negroes. I told the Colo-
> nel: 'Yes, sir, I know Negroes, a few of them, that I
> was raised among and who knew me and my fathers
> just as my fathers knew their fathers. I suppose, what
> you mean is, understand Negroes.' I told him I didn't
> know what there was he wanted understood about
> them; that maybe any human being was his own
> enigma which he would take with him to the grave,
> but I didn't know how the color of his skin was going
> to make that any clearer or more obscure.

> "So I took the company, along with the promotion (as
> you see, I am Captain Galloway now), and imagine
> me, sitting at the table in the P.C. and the orderly
> brings in the list of replacements and I look at it and
> the first name on it is—"

DISSOLVE TO:

A company Post of Command, a dugout, in the lines
in France. Sam, Junior, sits at the desk contrived of a
wooden box. His uniform is muddy, worn. Other officers, a signalman, runners, etc., in the scene, maps and

telephone, sound of gunfire outside. A runner enters, followed by a group of Negro soldiers temporarily commanded by Spoot, now a sergeant. Spoot and Sam, Junior, recognize each other; Spoot has been hunting for Sam, Junior, for a year now. But the matter is official yet. Sergeant Moxey turns his party over to the Captain. Sam dismisses them, asks Sergeant Moxey to return.

Spoot returns. Now he and Sam are alone. They are once more the two boys who fed from the same breast, who hunted the bird nest and stole the pig and were whipped for it, who slept in the same bed until after they were both so big that they would have to sleep together by stealth to keep old Rachel from catching them, who hunted together and had never been separated until Sam went to Yale. This is simply a reunion. We will play into it whatever is necessary. It shows mainly the relationship between these two men of different races, how little the difference in race means to them when they are alone.

Later, Sam, Junior, leads his company in a raid or an attack. When they return to the trench, Sam is missing. Spoot is grimly and coldly frantic. He finds a man who saw Sam fall. Spoot will go and get him. They forbid him, try to stop him. He slips out, anyway, crawls to the German lines in the darkness, under fire.

He hunts for Sam by the scar on his wrist which they got while kidnapping the pig. He finds Sam by this means. The Germans have heard Spoot, Very lights go up; they are under fire. Spoot cannot get back with Sam. He tries to cover Sam's body with his own as the machine gun bullets seek them out and kill them both.

DISSOLVE TO:

Old Sam's library. Sam, Edith, Caroline, Alice are gathered as the two telegrams arrive. CLOSE SHOT of first telegram:

> UNITED STATES OF AMERICA WAR DEPARTMENT
> . . . to inform you that your son, Captain Samuel B. Galloway—

LAP DISSOLVE TO:

. . . Sergeant Sam G. Moxey, was killed in action—

Sam and Caroline go to old Rachel to tell her. She is in bed. She is quite old, in a coma almost as Sam and Caroline lean over the bed.

SAM: Rachel.

Rachel opens her eyes. They look quietly at Sam; they do not know if she even sees him or not.

RACHEL: *(quietly)* Yes, Sam. I'm coming. *(she dies)*

DISSOLVE TO:

Negro voices singing a spiritual over DISSOLVE TO:
Sam's parlor, the big house. Rachel's funeral, Rachel in her coffin in state while the Negro choir sings. The family are gathered, a few white friends, old people who have known Rachel and Sam a long time. The dining-room door is open. It is filled with Negroes, standing.

When the spiritual ends, Sam stands at the head of the coffin. On a table behind him are photographs of Spoot and Sam, Junior, in uniform. Sam delivers the oration. (Will use one I delivered in like circumstances over an old Negro servant of my family.)

When Sam ceases, the choir leader gives signal. The choir sings another spiritual into —

FADE OUT.

VI

Time: 1941. Sam is about seventy. He has done well. He is as solid now as any man in the town. He could retire if he liked. But he is still active, still the champion of justice among the weak and helpless. But this is merely a hobby now.

Caroline is also about seventy. She is now what Rachel was. Spoot's wife is the cook, and now Caroline has only to run the house and train Edith's children as old Rachel had trained Sam, Junior, and Edith in their childhood.

Edith's first daughter is about twenty-three, married; old Sam is a great-grandfather. Her second child is the one who should have been a boy, whose birth they all waited for during the grief over Sam, Junior's, death. But the child was another girl. Nevertheless, she was named Sam Galloway Coldfield, called Lally, and she is a throwback.

She was not only a tomboy through her childhood and youth (she is seventeen now) but she is more like old Sam than any of the others have been. She has been old Sam's constant companion. There exists between them a rapport closer than that between twins, even. They seem almost to read each other's minds. It was she who hunted bird nests and snakes and stole pigs, etc., with Spoot's son, as Sam, Junior, and Spoot had done in their time, until old Sam put an end to it so that Lally could at least act like a girl now and then.

Carter Hoyt is about seventy. Margaret Hoyt has a son, twenty, Carter Hoyt Mitchell.

FADE IN

Voice on track over FADE IN:

. . . the old, old story of Montague and Capulet. But this time. . . .

It is the mild, late-fall Sunday afternoon when the news of Pearl Harbor reached the little southern towns like Jefferson. Carter Mitchell has to slip in the back way and meet Lally in the garden. They are modern young people, in definite contrast to Sam and Edith in their day, and to Sam, Junior, and Carter's mother in theirs.

Carter is trying to kiss Lally. She resists. She is not alarmed at all; she simply keeps her mouth away. It is like a wrestling bout, to see which is the better man.

CARTER: Come on, come on. If you don't know anything about kissing, do you want to wait all your life before you learn?

But Lally holds him off. Kissing's not important; time enough for that, etc. Carter gradually realizes that she is actually bargaining with him. He wants to know why. Finally he gets it that she wants him to agree that they will marry. He says that's easy to say: any man can say that to any girl. But he doesn't mean this. He and she both know that they are serious; that if they say it, they will mean it for always. He agrees, says all right, that's what he means, too. She lets him kiss her, a long kiss. He raises his head.

CARTER: Was it me or you that said you didn't know anything about kissing?

She doesn't answer, offering her mouth, waiting. He lowers his face again. Before they kiss, a sound behind them, a neighbor, a middle-aged snuffy excited man, bursts over the hedge. The radio has just told it: the Japs are bombing Pearl Harbor.

CARTER: What?

NEIGHBOR: The whole fleet's sunk!

The neighbor vanishes, carrying his frantic news. Lally has not moved, waiting for Carter to kiss her.

LALLY: Come on. You can't do anything about it today.

They kiss again, long kiss into —

DISSOLVE TO:

February, 1942. Bataan battle is going on. The family and the town are gradually awakening to what the country is faced with. Carter Mitchell is in school, at the State University in Oxford. He manages from time to time to come back to Jefferson, to see Lally. Their families do not know it. Lally meets Carter in her roadster between trains. Each time, Lally realizes it is becoming harder and harder for Carter to stay out of the war. But he is not yet twenty-one; his grandfather, who is his guardian, will not consent. Old Hoyt wants Carter to stay out of the war until he has to go, is drafted.

LALLY: Tell them you are twenty-one. Fake a birth certificate.

Carter says yes, that's what he will probably have to do since a man can't stay out of it forever.

Lally returns in her car, meets Spoot, Junior, as she is putting the car up. She says something about the war; how all the young men will have to go now. Spoot has been thinking about it. He says there is a squadron of Negroes being trained to fly at Tuskegee. That's what he would like to do, believes he can do. Lally asks him why he does not. He says it takes schooling.

LALLY: You graduated from high school.

SPOOT, JUNIOR: Yessum. But they want university men—

LALLY: That's just books. Get the books. I'll help you bone up on what you will need.

A month later. Lally and Carter meet again. Carter tells her he can't wait any longer; he has got a faked birth certificate, and he is going to enlist. Lally is not surprised. She expected that of him.

LALLY: All right. Kiss me, then.

DISSOLVE TO:

INT. CAROLINE'S CABIN   NIGHT

Caroline is sewing before the fire. Spoot, Junior, has books spread on the table under the lamp. Lally is helping him try to pass his entrance to Tuskegee. She works hard, but something is worrying her. She seems to forget now and then, become grave and thoughtful.

They notice it. Caroline watches Lally thoughtfully. Lally
rouses, goes on helping Spoot.

Lally manages to see Spoot alone. She asks him to send a telegram for her. It is to Carter. It says:

"YES. COME SOON AS YOU CAN."

LAP DISSOLVE TO:

A telegram from Carter to Lally:

"TONIGHT. SAME."

DISSOLVE TO:

Lally in her roadster meets a train at another station. Carter gets off. He is in uniform. He is hurried, grave. Lally is grave, too.

CARTER: Are you sure?

LALLY: That's hardly something I would joke about.

CARTER: All right. Let's get going. We've got two hours before the train goes back.

They wake a clerk up and get a wedding license. They are frantic at the clerk's deliberation as Carter watches his watch. At last they have the license. Then they can't find anyone available to marry them. Perhaps a convention, ministers away, etc., or some other circumstance they could not have anticipated and for which they have no recourse in the time left. If Carter misses this train, he will be absent without leave, his father may hear of it and find him and jerk him back home. But there is nothing else to do; he will have to go absent. They must find someone to marry them. But Lally refuses. She will not hear of it; he must not worry about her. He must get back to his post before the time is up. Carter makes one last effort. He talks to a night filling-station man. The man tells them of a country J.P. who lives on the road leading to the next station. By driving fast, they can just barely reach the J.P., be married, then race the train on to the next station and catch it there.

This is the last chance. They take it. They race to the J.P.'s house, find he is gone or sick or not available. While they stand at the door they hear the train passing. They rush back to the car, race the train to the next station and reach there just in time for Carter to board it.

Lally returns home. It is late. Old Sam has the household aroused, waiting for her. When she returns at last, the relief of his anxiety becomes rage. He creates a scene. Lally has gone through a certain amount of strain herself. This is complicated by her physical condition. To her own shame, in the middle of the scene she faints, collapses. Caroline and Alice take her to her room, put her to bed. Caroline sends Alice away. It does not take Caroline long to divine what is wrong with Lally. She soothes Lally, quiets her to sleep.

The next morning Caroline goes to old Sam, who is waiting to know what is wrong. He does not suspect the truth for one moment, until he learns it from Caroline. Old Sam blows his top at once. He breathes fire and brimstone. He will go first to old Carter Hoyt. Then he will take his pistol and go to the University and attend to young Carter. Caroline tells him young Carter is not at the University, is a soldier now. Then old Sam will go and straighten out old Carter Hoyt. Alice has heard the uproar. She enters. She and Caroline try to stop old Sam, but they cannot. He goes charging out to see old Carter Hoyt.

Caroline goes up to Lally's room. Lally is awake, but she still feels pretty shaky. It is too bad that she should have to be bothered at this time. But she realizes that only she can do anything now. She gets up.

LALLY: The old fool! Couldn't you stop him?

Caroline helps her to dress. She and Caroline leave in pursuit of old Sam.

Spoot, Junior, has enlisted. He is not there to drive the car. Old Sam has shouted and raged until Tobe, an old man now, has got the old surrey out. Old Sam is driven to the Hoyt house in the surrey, storms in and finds old Carter Hoyt in his library. Hoyt is still an invalid, wears his dressing gown.

A scene between the two old men who have been bitter enemies for almost fifty years. They have not spoken on the street. Twenty-five years ago, old Sam made the sacrifice and went to Hoyt, willing to apologize for the sake of their children, and was repulsed and insulted. He has returned now in righteous rage to vindicate the good name of his daughter.

This is old Hoyt's chance for complete triumph over his old enemy. He thinks young Carter is at the University. When Sam divulges what has happened, Hoyt says he is not at all surprised at a Galloway behaving like this; he is only surprised that a Hoyt should have so demeaned himself. This scene will be two furious and impotent old men, clinging to their old dead angers and standards. It will be in absolute and direct contrast to

the later ones between the old men and the young
people, with their young beliefs and their hard modern
conceptions of truths which they have learned: how the
old people with their outdated ideas and lack of honesty
and courage have brought about the modern world
which the young now have to face and solve, to save not
only themselves but the old, too.

In the scene, old Hoyt learns for the first time that
young Carter is not in the University but is now a soldier. Before he can react to this, Lally and Caroline
enter. Lally takes charge, shuts her grandfather up and
takes him away and gets him back home, leaving old
Hoyt shocked and amazed at what he has just learned
about his grandson. Old Hoyt is now shouting for his
conveyance, to follow Lally and Sam.

The uproar is now transferred to Sam's library. Sam
and Lally and Caroline and Alice. Old Sam is still raging, or trying to, until Lally stops him dead in his tracks.
He realizes that she is not angry, is not ashamed nor
even frightened. She is calm, talks to him as if he were
an hysterical child almost. She tells him a few truths. He
gets a new picture of young people of 1942, who have
the courage of their mistakes and bottom and even
pride and an ability to face truth which old Sam begins
to realize that perhaps he has not. She tells him calmly
how it was the old people like him, with their greed and
blundering and cowardice and folly, who brought on
this war, brought about this situation in which Carter
and Spoot, Junior, will have to risk their lives and perhaps lose them, as her Uncle Sam and Spoot, Junior's,
father did in the last war. She tells old Sam to hold his
horses; she and Carter have never intended anything

else but to get married, and so preserve the family's good name that old Sam seems so anxious about. They don't need anybody's consent to do that.

LALLY: I like you, and Carter even likes old Mr. Hoyt, though I can't see why. But we don't need yours or his sanction, either. It's Carter and me that want to room together and love one another and have fun working and raising children—as soon as he and the rest of the young men can get done fighting Japs and Germans.

Old Sam is speechless with amazement, is convinced by her very calmness and courage that perhaps young people do know what they are doing.

At this point old Hoyt comes storming in. He demands to know where his grandson is. Carter will not be twenty-one until next year; he will have him discharged for misrepresenting his age and having no guardian's consent to enlist. Only Lally knows where Carter is. She flatly refuses to tell old Hoyt. Hoyt then tries to bargain. He says that if Lally will tell him where Carter is, help him get Carter out of the army, to wait until he is drafted, old Hoyt will give his consent to the wedding. Lally calmly tells old Hoyt nobody needs his consent to the wedding. Hoyt appeals to Sam. He offers Sam the chance to preserve his daughter's good name, etc. But old Sam is for Lally, even if he cannot quite yet reconcile and understand it. But he knows guts when he sees it.

He tells old Hoyt: How can two outdated stupid old men like them save the good name of people who are already braver and stronger than they have ever been? What is there that such old men can do, that these young people can need? Maybe he is too old to be as brave as

Lally, but Lally has enough guts for her grandfather to share, too, and Sam hopes that Carter will share some of his guts with his grandfather. He (old Sam), speaking ironically now, hopes that a soldier will have enough courage to share even with a damned old man like Hoyt, and even if Carter hasn't enough, then, by God, his granddaughter Lally will have enough for all of them.

Old Hoyt realizes he is beaten, by this young girl who should have been cringing and weeping in shame, but who has not even lost her temper.

> **HOYT:** *(humbly almost, to Lally)* I want to see Carter. I'm an old man. I may not be here when he reaches twenty-one and will come back to see me. Will you let me see him?

> **LALLY:** Yes. Just write the letter giving him your permission to enlist. That's all we want.

Hoyt agrees.

DISSOLVE TO:

Some time has elapsed, a month, maybe more. Spoot, Junior, is home on leave, a sergeant. Carter is home on leave, especial leave to get married. The wedding takes place in the church. Caroline, Alice and Spoot are in a pew at the back of the white church. Old Sam and old Hoyt sit side by side in a pew, stiff and unbending, still ready to breathe fire at one another, observing an armistice during the ceremony simply for decency's sake.

That night. Old Sam is in the yard, watching the lighted window of Lally and Carter's room until the light goes off. He is proud, triumphant, yet quiet, happy. He sees a shadow, finds that Caroline is watching the window, too. The light goes out. Caroline approaches Sam.

CAROLINE: You come on in now, out of this night air.

Old Sam follows obediently in.

DISSOLVE TO:

The continuation of the opening scene, in which Sam, Hoyt, Caroline and Lally are in the library when the two soldiers, Spoot, Junior, and Carter, enter to say good-bye. Sam, Hoyt, Lally and Caroline stand at the top of the front steps, Sam's arm about Lally, as the four of them look down at Spoot and Carter, who are about to leave. Carter and Spoot turn and start walking down the drive.

CARTER: *(to Spoot)* Come on, Sergeant. Pick it up.

Spoot skips step to pace with Carter. They go on.

CAROLINE: *(turns)* Supper's ready.

CLOSE GROUP SHOT AT FRONT DOOR

Sam and Hoyt pause. Now they begin to breathe fire.

HOYT: *(to Sam)* After you.

SAM: After you. Go on.

Caroline opens the door, waits while Sam and Hoyt glare at each other.

HOYT: Maybe your girl did marry that damn boy, but I still won't break bread with you.

SAM: You can't! I'm going to have my supper in my bedroom!

CAROLINE: Yawl go on to the dining room and set down to your supper, now. Go on.

Sam and Hoyt enter the house. Caroline holds the door. Lally enters, stops, turns, looking back at Carter. Caroline passes her, pauses.

CAROLINE: Come on, honey. Don't nobody care whether them two eats or not, but you got to eat. Come on, now.

Lally turns with Caroline. They walk into the house in —

FADE OUT.

THE END

The Life and Death of a Bomber

(It arrived too late, and so died.)

ACT I
It is going to be too late.
(This should not happen)

Smith is an Air Force officer, a civilian engineer and an army-trained pilot, who has been assigned to a bomber factory to observe the assembling and conduct the final testing of a new bomber. He is a civilian, who has become a soldier only in his country's hours of need.

After reaching the city, and before reporting to the factory, he meets a strange young woman. They are attracted to each other immediately. He realizes that the woman likes him, but she is trying to brush him off and escape. He does not know why. He holds her only long enough to learn that she is married, her husband is a bomber-factory foreman, and that she works too. He takes this to mean she is a secretary or something of that nature. But she escapes from him before he can learn any more.

Smith reports to the factory. Because of his civilian avocation, he has not only a pilot's but an engineer's interest and understanding of what the factory is doing. The bomber is a new series, first production job, which

if successful will be the forerunner of fleets of new and
efficient bombers which will shorten and end the war
and so save the lives of many American troops. The
entire factory has concentrated on this one bomber;
managers, superintendents, shop foremen and workmen, to produce it as efficiently and as quickly as possible, to turn out the best bomber yet. A deadline has been
set for its completion and everyone in the plant has an
interest and a part in the job.

Smith is conducted on a preliminary trip to follow the
bomber's evolution from a blueprint to the finished
airplane ready to fly. As he follows his guides, he recognizes in one of the assembly lines the young woman he
met this morning. She recognizes him, too. When they
look at each other this time, it seems to Smith that an
electric shock passed between them. He believes she felt
it, too. He did not know where she worked, but he
realizes now that she must have known all the time
where he was going and that they would meet again. She
could have avoided seeing him again by quitting her job,
yet she didn't. That she did not, that she should be
working in the very factory to which he has been assigned by war orders, seems to him a notification from
fate that they are to change each other's life, and that she
must know this and accept it, too. He goes on, listening
to his guides.

He completes this first inspection tour. By indirect
inquiry he learns when the shifts will change and how to
see the woman; he may even learn here who she is, who
her husband is. He waits for her. She is not surprised.
She expected it. She still resists, even though she knows
there is something here she can't escape and doesn't

want to. But she wants it done decently, some decent solution, not only for her sake but for her husband's, who is doing an important war-job. She will not upset him, impair his efficiency at this time. Smith has no pity for the husband who can't keep his wife, but he recognizes the husband's important present job, and he loves the woman and will do what she wants, but it must not be too long away. He allows her to go on.

He continues to examine into all phases of bomber construction. The workmen realize that he is a trained engineer, knows what he is talking about and can understand their language and problems. They know that he has the same aim as they: to build good bombers and build them quickly. They accept him, give him any information he wants.

One day he finds a workman who has invented a scheme, an idea, a minor change, which, if used, would shorten the construction time of each bomber by a certain number of minutes. Multiply these lost minutes by so many bombers, and this wasted time would have been sufficient to have produced one more complete bomber in the same time. Smith wants to know why the idea has not been put into use. At first they won't tell him. He insists on an answer. Finally they tell him that they cannot pass the foreman with the new idea. He keeps on at them, and learns that this situation occurs in all factories, ones in war production and not.

SMITH: But in a factory like this one, in war production, this is serious.

A WORKMAN: It's serious in any of them.

Smith realizes that there is something here which they

are concealing even from him, with which the workmen do not trust even him. He says he will go to the superintendent and tell him of the idea. He, Smith, is an impartial observer; he can report the idea without naming any names, etc., and so will compromise no one. But they ask him not to. They will not tell him why.

SMITH: Well, you certainly can't stop me from asking Mr. Halliday the reason.

Halliday, the foreman, learns about the situation between his wife and the army pilot. He learns it unexpectedly, by accident. They are on different shifts, and do not see one another very often. When he sees her at last, he sees something different in her. She seems both unhappier and yet happier at the same time. There is something strained about her, something shining and different, yet grave. She has not been trying to hide it from her husband; they have just not had a chance yet to talk, and, as she told Smith, she does not want to worry her husband until the bomber is finished. But Halliday learns about it. Perhaps Smith has given the wife a token of some sort—a badge from his collar, or his good luck emblem he wears when he flies. Halliday finds it. The wife tells him about Smith, that maybe they are in love, she doesn't know for sure, but there is something, but she will do nothing to hurt Halliday, is sorry he had to learn it now. She has not decided what she will do yet, but whatever she decides, she will try to be fair and decent with him.

Halliday restrains himself. He must be careful too, not to drive her to Smith out of hand. They go to the factory to work. The wife seeks Smith out at once, tells him the husband knows. Smith says, "Fine, now we don't need to wait and hide, etc." But she stops him there. Nothing is settled yet. The bomber must be finished first. She goes on to work.

Now the situation is changed between Smith and the husband. Smith had intended to meet the husband only over the question of building bombers faster. Now there is another element in it. But he goes to Halliday, asks him why the new idea is not used. Halliday wants to know what business it is of Smith's, tells him not to meddle in what does not concern him and that this advice can go for a lot of other things too. Smith restrains himself. He is doing the husband an injury to begin with; for the wife's sake he does not intend to fight with Halliday yet. Halliday sees Smith is determined to keep his temper. Halliday pulls himself up too. He tells Smith, "Come on then, if you want to know why."

He takes Smith unofficially to a conference between the labor heads and their lawyers, and the lawyers and representatives of the factory owners. Smith discovers what is the true bottleneck in war production. Labor is not refusing to speed up production simply because they will not be paid extra for it. They are merely trying to protect themselves. They have struggled a hundred years to gain better work and pay conditions. They are now being asked to discard this gain because of the national emergency. That is all right. They are willing to sacrifice them, produce more, and so increase the profits of what they produce. But the stockholders shall not keep those extra profits to add to the profits which they already draw from the production without doing any of the work.

Labor is willing to increase production without extra pay, provided the stockholders will give the extra profits from it to the government. This the stockholders will not agree to do. Thus the stockholders spread the rumors that labor is holding up the war for selfish reasons. Smith learns that the working men who do the work and the white collar men who superintend it could get together without trouble, but are stymied from one another by the representatives of the two factions, labor and capital, who are concerned first in protecting the establishments which they represent. Smith and Halliday leave the meeting.

HALLIDAY: Well? Are you satisfied now?

Smith has no answer. Halliday leaves him. Smith talks to an old workman.

SMITH: While you people are squabbling about who gets the money, soldiers are dying.

WORKMAN: Some of them are our sons, too.

SMITH: And they die, too.

WORKMAN: Yes. But at least our sons die so that their kin and descendants will have a better world to work and earn their bread in: not just to increase and preserve the cash which their parents did not even work to earn.

Smith tries to find the wife. She has gone home. He follows her there. He has promised he would never come to the house, to give her freedom and time to plan what she will do about the situation. He tells her what sort of man her husband is: who would sabotage war production at this crucial time? She defends her husband, to the extent that at least he believes he is doing right for the sake of labor, the men from whom he rose, etc. Both of them are excited, worked up. So far she has held him off, until she can settle matters. The scene ends with them in their first embrace. At this moment Halliday enters. He knew where Smith would be going, and so followed also.

This is the blowoff. Halliday learns that his wife loves Smith, or thinks she does, or at least intends to act on that idea. Smith leaves. Halliday asks his wife again if she means it. She tells him she does, had wanted to keep the matter down until the bomber was finished, not to distract her husband. When the scene ends, they have agreed on a separation for the time being, even though they live in the same house and must continue to do so until the work is finished. Halliday does not insist. He is on delicate ground; he has lost too much: a false move, and he will lose his wife.

Now he must do something to keep her. He will get rid of Smith by finishing the bomber as quickly as possible. Then Smith will test it, and will have to leave, will be ordered somewhere else, etc. This is the only hope Halliday can see. Once Smith must leave, perhaps he can dissuade his wife, win her back. But he must still stick to his principles about protecting labor from the people whom he believes are exploiting it; he certainly cannot keep his self-respect and at the same time throw his principles overboard just to keep his wife. So his only recourse is to speed up production itself on this one bomber, put the pressure on the workmen, to speed up production not of all bombers but only of this particular one. He challenges the workmen in his section to try to cut some more time yet off the deadline for finishing the bomber. The men are willing to make the extra effort. One man suggests that they might use the workman's new idea and speed up all the bombers, but the men find out quickly that this is not Halliday's plan yet. But they are willing to bear down and get the bomber out ahead of schedule.

Halliday keeps his section going at top speed, taking up a tool here and there himself when he finds a temporary slowdown. A slight error occurs. Halliday catches it almost at once. He decides swiftly. To correct it now would lose a certain amount of time. The error may not be serious, can be corrected later, may not show at all during the test. After that it can be removed, no harm done and nobody the wiser. He lets it pass, the bomber is finished and rolled out for test a day ahead of schedule.

Smith has been helping, too, doing what he can and whatever they will allow him, to get the bomber out. He and Halliday have concealed their private feelings during the speed-up. But Smith knows that Halliday has passed the error.

The bomber is ready for testing. The factory and the army officials arrive to watch the test. Smith is now formally in command of the bomber, with a factory pilot as his second, and other factory men as a checking and inspection crew during the test. Smith approaches Halliday, who formally turns the bomber over to him as checked and airworthy. Smith and Halliday are alone for a moment. Smith tells Halliday that this is one way, certainly, for Halliday to solve his family problems, but has Halliday been thorough enough to fix Smith's parachute, too? Halliday then tells Smith that he has got permission and is going along on the test flight, too.

Smith, Halliday and the crew board the bomber, and Smith takes it off. He puts it through the test, and comes in to land. He puts the gear down, but it will not lock into down position. He gains altitude again and circles the field while Halliday climbs down into (wings? bomb bay? will check) to see what is wrong. He finds the trouble, but he cannot fix it, returns and reports to Smith. Smith orders all the others to jump. They obey him, until only Halliday is left. Smith orders Halliday to leave the ship, so he can make a crash landing, save what he can of it, if it doesn't catch fire. For reply, Halliday throws his parachute out; if Smith will stay with the ship, he will, too. In that case, Smith says, they had better see what can be done about the gear. He puts the automatic pilot on, starts to get out of his parachute. Halliday reaches over, pulls out a wire that puts the automatic out of commission, so that Smith will have to fly the plane. Halliday tells Smith to make the landing, and Halliday climbs back down to the jammed gear and tries to wedge it locked with a tool or whatever (will check). Smith makes the landing. The gear collapses, crushes Halliday's hand off. The bomber stops on its belly, props and flaps, etc., bent, stops finally as, for all practical purposes, a crack-up.

The next day Smith and the wife meet in Halliday's hospital room. Instead of gaining a day, the bomber has lost three. Halliday has lost his hand, is maimed for life as far as war production is concerned, all because of the mistakes which the three of them brought about. They

are all to blame. Smith and the wife still feel the same
attraction for one another, but it is as if the bomber
wrecked on the field has come between them forever; a
warning, a silent demand that they forget themselves for
its sake so that it and the bombers to follow it can get on
with the war, can sacrifice themselves for something
worthwhile. Smith tells Halliday goodbye. The wife follows him from the room, they say farewell, Smith departs. The wife goes back to her husband. Halliday asks
the superintendent to come to him. Halliday tells the
superintendent about the workman's idea to shorten
production time. It is to be put into effect at once.

The wrecked bomber is being repaired as quickly as
possible. The whole factory is now trying to make up as
much as possible of the lost time.

ACT II
It is too late.
(This is happening)

The bomber is repaired. By putting everything else
aside and all working together, the factory has managed
to repair the bomber in a day and a half instead of two
days. Thus it is now only a day and a half late.

But the squadron of bombers with which it was to fly
in a sort of convoy out to the battle front has gone on
and left it. The ferry crew has come to take it out to the
front. While they are getting final instructions in the
office, someone shouts, they look out the window toward the tarmac where the bomber is waiting, and it is
moving, rolling slowly along the apron. (We can use an

unusual wind, if necessary.) Mechanics overtake it, stop it, the pilot and others get in to see what is wrong. The bomber is empty, engines not running, the brakes are set up and locked for parking, as they should be. Yet the bomber began to move, as if it knew itself that it was late, and was trying to get on. The men are puzzled. They examine the brakes. They are all right. They lock them. This time they stay locked. They can find nothing wrong. Yet the bomber of its own accord had moved.

The weather reports show a storm area moving east across the Pacific. But they will have time to reach Hawaii, the first refueling point, before they touch the storm, and so will not have to worry about that yet. If they had not lost the day and a half, they would probably be able to miss it altogether. But they will worry about the storm when they reach Hawaii.

The bomber takes off. While in flight the two pilots notice how it is running: the engines seem stronger, the plane is traveling faster than they expected, than it was even intended to, etc. (We further the idea that the bomber itself is trying its best to overcome its handicap.)

They reach Hawaii, refuel, check out again. The storm is closer. They will have to either go through it, or wait until it passes.

A PILOT: The old gal's already lost two days. She flew rings around herself coming out and picked up three hours. But she's still late. We'll go on.

SECOND PILOT: Yes, we mustn't let her down, trying like she is. She's already cost a man his hand; if she's trying to make it up, we'll help her.

They take off again. They enter the storm. The instruments go wrong from electricity, static, etc. They are blown off-course. The navigator plots them out of the storm. When he can establish their position, they have only enough fuel left to possibly reach a small island. It is doubtful if they will even reach this.

(Will research, make this plausible.) The navigator feels that their predicament is his fault. He is acquainted with this part of the world—can be a native of Hawaii, etc.—so he knows of a trading steamer or some such which used to make regular trips on a regular course here. He believes this is the only chance the crew will have to ever get off the island, if they can reach it.

He does not tell the pilot what he intends to do, because he knows the pilot would refuse him permission. So he takes the job on himself, gets a gunner to help him. The navigator assures himself that the pilot has the correct course for the island. Then he and the gunner drop an inflatable raft from the plane, the navigator follows it by parachute, guides his descent so that he strikes the water near the raft, inflates it and climbs into it to wait in the hopes of having the little steamer find him when and if it passes. (Will be careful about this, to prevent hoakum.)

DISSOLVE TO:

Tiny island. A clearing hardly big enough for anything to land in it. The bomber is out of gas. The plane sideslips, performs the impossible, gets into the clearing, ground-loops, stops at last with its nose thrust into the jungle at the other end of the clearing.

CLOSE   INT. COCKPIT

The bomber has stopped, a few tree limbs thrust into the cockpit, into the pilots' faces. The first pilot draws a deep breath, turns to the second pilot.

PILOT: Jesus, what a landing you made. But what in hell do you mean, taking the ship away from me?

SECOND PILOT: I didn't take it.

FIRST PILOT: You didn't touch the controls?

SECOND PILOT: No. I swear I didn't touch them.

They get out of the ship, look at it. It is intact. It has landed in a place so small as to be impossible, unbelievable. The pilots are quiet, amazed.

FIRST PILOT: *(dreamily)* What do you call those little popguns? Those little monoplanes with four cylinders and nothing inside but a stick and a throttle and a dollar watch?

SECOND PILOT: Cubs.

FIRST PILOT: Yeah. Cubs.

The pilot realizes that the crew will go to pieces if they remain idle to think about their hopeless outlook. So he puts them to work. He is harsh and sharp, divides them into squads, some to hunt food, others he sets to work clearing and leveling the runway which they cannot use without gasoline and which they will probably never be able to use. He knows what the navigator has done now. He asks his men which they had rather do: perform a little work together, or be sitting out there in the ocean by themselves like Jake is now?

One day they discover that they are being watched, and are practically prisoners. But they never see the savages. A man hunting in the woods finds a dart sticking suddenly in a tree beside him, is driven back to the clearing. Another finds himself in a crude trap, barely manages to get out of it.

They find themselves hemmed in to the clearing. They realize that the savages could kill them at any time, but for some reason have not, that they are being starved to death where they are because they can't go into the jungle to hunt. A gunner goes off his head from the strain, thinks he hears something in the jungle, rushes into the jungle before the others can stop him, with his pistol. The others hear the shots, growing fainter and fainter as the man runs on. The shots cease at last. A search party is organized. They find the man dead from a poisoned dart. While they stand over the body, other darts fall about them. They realize that these darts are deliberate misses, merely warnings to drive them back to the clearing.

They hold a council that night. Something must be done. If they could only get in communication with the savages, they might do something about it. Apparently what the savages want is to capture one of them alive for some reason. As it is, they are virtually prisoners, and if they keep on like this, they will starve. At last the co-pilot rises. If that's what they want, they will get it. He will walk into the jungle and see what will happen. They all realize that he may come back, but probably won't; that he may stay alive, but maybe he won't either. The co-pilot walks to the edge of the jungle, they watch him. He turns, looks back at them. He makes a flippant salute.

CO-PILOT: So long, guys. Keep your noses clean.

He enters the jungle, disappears.

The little trading steamer finds the rubber raft floating in the sea. The navigator is gone, but he has left a message telling where the bomber is.

A cargo plane finds the island and the landing field, brings food and fuel, the bomber gets away at last. It has now cost the lives of three men, as well as the foreman's hand.

ACT III
It was too late.
(This must never happen again)

The bomber has reached the front. It is a temporary base to which our forces have retreated because not enough bombers had arrived soon enough. We have paused here to get breath, collect ourselves and retreat again. An enemy task force is pursuing us. We must evacuate this point soon or we will be caught.

The lone bomber is the only aircraft we have at this point to intervene and slow up the approaching enemy force. It is being sent out to delay the enemy as much as possible, so we can escape. The attempt will be suicidal. A volunteer crew has been got together to take the bomber out. The moment is grave. The names of the crew are written in chalk on the operations office bulletin board. One member of it is the son of a workman of the factory which made the bomber. Another is the son of a wealthy stockholder in the factory. We have here sons of the two factions whose refusal to meet one another caused the delay in bomber production. The bomber takes off to try to delay the enemy. The ground forces pack up to move again. The bulletin board is taken down and packed also to be moved.

The bomber departs. It has aboard all the fuel which existed at the base; even if there is enough gas to get it back to the base after the attack, there will be no more fuel waiting to enable it to escape, follow the retreating troops which it has saved.

The enemy force is finally sighted. The pilots know that there is not enough fuel left now to get them back to the base, back to land even. But they attack, are attacked by screening fighters. They make one run, drop bombs, sink a vessel, are attacked by more enemy fighters, the bombardier is killed, no one else can operate the bomb sight. The pilot makes a low-level run, practically dive-bombing. Fighters swarm about them, another gunner is killed, the bomber has no rear protection anymore. Nevertheless, it continues to make the final bombing run. It drops its last bomb, the co-pilot is killed, the pilot pulls out, straightens out again. Fighters swarm over it, shooting it to pieces as it struggles on, bombs and ammunition and fuel all gone now. The fighters still swarm over it.

CLOSE SHOT from pilot's window of one wing, two engines, enemy bullets going into the wing; oil from the engines begins to flow backward across the wing like the bomber's blood in —

FADE OUT.

The new base to which our forces have been able to retreat. They have met reinforcements and have consolidated and are now safe, because of the bomber's gallant action. Our offensive is about to open. Headquarters is being set up. The bulletin board is unpacked, the chalked names of the dead bomber-crews have become blurred in the moving. The orderly asks the officer what to do about the blurred names. The officer says, Erase them; new names are waiting to go up. The orderly erases the old names, writes in the new ones; other bombers depart to attack the enemy. The adjutant listens until the sound dies away. Then he turns back to his official report which will be cabled to Washington.

DISSOLVE TO:

Washington. Telegrams are being sent to notify the families of the dead airmen. Two clerks happen to notice how the three airmen who were lost in the Pacific were in the same plane in which these last seven men died. They are curious for a moment at the coincidence, wonder what story might lie behind it, probably nothing of interest, go on with their work.

DISSOLVE TO:

The ferry pilot of the Pacific island episode is back home on his first leave. He goes to the home of his co-pilot's widowed mother, tells her about her dead son. He tells her how first the navigator and then her son had given their lives to try to save the others and the bomber, and that the bomber had got on to do its job, to save at least some other lives that without it might have been lost. He tells her he has been ordered to report to the factory which built the bomber, to tell the people who created it that it had done its job and they had done the best they could to help it, so that the men at the factory would know that the airmen themselves would not let them down, were ready to take all risks they could to use to advantage the tools which the factories were working to produce.

DISSOLVE TO:

The bomber factory. A new batch of bombers has just been completed and is about to depart. A general send-off is being held, an open-air mass meeting. The one-handed foreman, the two fathers of the dead airmen, the rich stockholder in his fine clothes and the mechanic in overalls, the ferry pilot are on the platform. The chairman tells how, because the factory used an idea invented by a workman in the factory, the plant is now turning out eleven bombers where it used to turn out only ten. Then the chairman says that foreman Halliday wants to say something to them.

Halliday comes to the mike. He is no speaker, would not have attempted it for any other reason or occasion. But he manages to get his own sincerity across to the listeners. He tells the story of a bomber that arrived too late, because the people who made it let their private selfish motives intervene; they failed where the young men who died to fly the bomber had no opportunity or choice to let their private wishes intervene between them and the risk of death and the job to be done. This must never happen again.

> **HALLIDAY:** I'm not speaking just to us, here. I'm talk-
> ing to all America, to all the men who are building the
> guns and planes and ships.

He then introduces a man who knows what he has been

trying to say, because the man has lived it, suffered it. He introduces the ferry pilot, who in turn delivers his message: that the airmen who risk death don't have to ask the men who make the planes to forego everything but the building of planes, because the young airmen never for a moment believe that the builders will do anything else but give everything to production. He finishes, stops. The new bombers take off and depart. Halliday takes the mike, tells the shift to go back to work.

FADE OUT.

THE END

The Damned Don't Cry

Savannah. Zelda's father is doing a carpentering job at Captain Middleton's house. Zelda was born on the wrong side of town, shanty Irish. But she is ambitious to better herself, dreams of decency, etc. She has taken the fine Middleton house as a symbol of all she doesn't have and dreams of for herself and her family, too. There is a very close sympathy between Zelda and her father, who is a chronic drunkard to the world, though to Zelda always a charming and understanding companion.

They return by river boat. Zelda meets Dan Carter. They are both about sixteen. Dan is the aristrocrat to her. He was born to what she dreams of—not money, but background. They talk, then separate. Dan goes ashore with his aunt, who to Zelda is a queen; they are met by a carriage while Zelda and her father walk home, carrying the carpenter tools. It was an incident of sheer chance, they will probably never meet again.

Zelda's home. Her mother is a harridan, a sloven, her brother an incipient criminal and degenerate. Following a sordid row with her mother and brother, Zelda puts on the angel costume she wore in a pageant in childhood. Her father staggers into the house, drunk, collapses. Zelda rushes down to him in the angel's costume and runs to fetch a doctor, but too late. Her father is dead.

The family is now without money or food. Her

mother is moaning and complaining at her hard luck and at Zelda's curious ungrateful ways, etc., the brother Lathe is doing nothing at all to help. Zelda goes to Captain Middleton and gets Lathe a job and also the promise of a job for herself as soon as she graduates from school in the spring. Her mother has taken to drink, and now Zelda runs the house, keeps Lathe at his job in spite of his grousing and the mother's complaining, and keeps up with her schoolwork, carrying the whole load, still confident although she loses patience with her mother and brother at times, but still true to her fierce ambition to better them all, make them be something. But she is beginning to lose all faith in her mother.

Lathe is caught by Middleton's superintendent stealing. Lathe comes to Zelda and confesses, begs her to see the manager or he will go to jail; wheedles Zelda: she can fix it up, either with the manager or, better, Captain Middleton, since she has a drag with him. Zelda refuses, through shame of her brother, to bother Middleton, but she allows Lathe to arrange for her to see the manager, who has already put the eye on her, as Lathe knows though she does not.

The manager talks Zelda along without committing himself, persuades her to go out to Tybee Beach with him. She sees which way the wind is setting, but she must try to keep Lathe out of jail, and she is confident she can take care of herself; anyway, she must risk it. He finally gets her off alone on the beach and sets out to assault her by force. She fights him off, escapes and outruns him. In a violent reaction from fear and disgust, she wants to cleanse herself physically. She finds a lonely part of the beach and takes off her clothes and goes swimming, finds a man also swimming, gets out of the water and into her clothes again. After the man dresses, they meet. It is Tyler. He makes no attempt to touch her, does not even seem curious as to who she is or why she is there. Her reaction from the other experience carries her toward him and, particularly as he is a good deal of an innocent liar, he soon becomes the knightly figure of the "aristocrat" of her dreams. They make a date to meet again.

Zelda goes to Captain Middleton, has the charges against Lathe quashed for her father's sake, although Lathe loses his job. Again there are sordid constant rows between Zelda and her mother and brother. But Zelda is still impervious to them, not only busy preparing to graduate but thinking of Tyler, waiting to meet him again.

The day comes when she and Tyler meet again. They go on a picnic to the old fort. Zelda is seduced.

Graduation night. Tyler is to meet her at the school. When she arrives, he is not there. She gets through the ceremony. When everybody has left the school and the lights are turned off, Tyler is still not there. When she reaches home, she finds a note from Tyler telling her goodbye, that he has gone to sea.

Zelda has now taken her promised job with Middleton. She is efficient. She persuades Middleton to give Lathe another chance, as an oiler on one of his boats: a job where Lathe can't steal anything. When she returns to her office, she has a fainting spell. A doctor tells her she is pregnant.

She doesn't know what to do. She has no friend save

Middleton, and she can't tell him. While sitting on a park bench, she meets Teppie Strickland, a prostitute who grew up in her neighborhood. Teppie is a good soul, kind and generous. Teppie suggests an abortion. Zelda will not hear of it. Then Teppie offers to find a home to take the child, asks Zelda what she will do meanwhile. Zelda is independent, not whipped yet, says she will take care of that part, just so the baby will be all right when it comes. She returns to Middleton and resigns her job. She refuses to tell him why, and asks him only to give her another job, any sort of job, in his organization somewhere else, in another town or port, where she will be asked no questions. He begins to smell a rat, but she refuses to tell him any more, faces him courageously, asking nothing but a chance to work. He agrees, and promises to stall Mrs. O'Brien off if she tries to find where Zelda is.

Mobile. Zelda has a job, a harder one, in bad surroundings: a tough waterfront setup. She passes for a wife whose husband is gone, dead or left her, she doesn't say. She sends money to her mother each month, is saving all she can toward the child's arrival. She meets Engstaad, a rum-runner. He is a hard man; he has to be. He sees at once Zelda's honesty and courage and character. He is like Tyler in that he never once makes an attempt at her, as all the other men with whom she is now thrown do. Instead, he is quite gentle, does little favors for her. He thinks her husband has run out on her, asks her to live with him. She is moved by his consideration and kindness, but she still has the dream which the Middleton house symbolizes in her mind. She tells him about the child to discourage him. He says that's all right; he will look out for the child, too. Then she tries to tell him about her ambition for decency, background. He can't understand that, but if she feels that way, it must be true; anyway it's O.K. He hasn't given up hope. His manner toward her does not change. One night she is able to help him save a load of liquor, shows courage, quick thinking, etc. He asks her to marry him, offers to quit rum-running, do whatever she likes. She declines. He wishes her well; if there is ever any time she needs him, etc.

The child is born. She puts it in an orphanage in Atlanta, and returns to Savannah.

She now has her old job back. She still tells Middleton nothing, nor her mother, despite the mother's nagging. Lathe has lost the second job and now drives a taxi. He has gone still more to pieces; Zelda realizes now that Lathe, too, is hopeless.

Captain Middleton dies. His house is to be sold. She goes to look at it for what may be the last time before strangers come into it. She meets Carter, who is the lawyer-agent for the estate. They recognize one another: the boy and girl from the boat. They are attracted to one another. Carter recognizes Zelda's character, her fierce aversion to falsity and smugness and such. Zelda sees in him the aristocrat, with background and gentility and grace, even though she sees his weaknesses: his lack of ambition, his willingness to condone injustice rather than struggle against it, his backward-looking toward the dead past and veneration of family merely because it is old. She sets out to buck him up, make him ambitious to improve himself and the world, too. To her, he was born with so much that he should try himself to attain all the rest: to become morally and mentally what he is by physical accident. She begins to wake him up, though he is still pulled the other way by his raising and background, which is represented by his aunt, who is afraid he will marry Zelda. Zelda finally persuades Carter to take without pay the case of a falsely accused, dissolute and penniless Negro. When Carter's aunt learns of this, she believes the worst has happened and that her nephew is now in Zelda's toils.

News of the first rape attempt spreads through the town.

Lathe is now cadging money from Zelda. He does not even pretend to work. She has given up all hope for him now. But he is still her brother. She corresponds regularly with the orphanage. She receives a photograph of her son, keeps it hidden with the letters in her locked drawer.

Engstaad has followed her to Savannah. He is in the money, getting rich, hard and tough still; he has to be. Yet with Zelda he is still gentle and dependable and still wants her under any condition, but still does not push himself, does not annoy her. He asks her again to marry him. He can quit now, buy the house she told him about and set up as gentlefolks. She declines again, gently. He says he understands, knows the other guy is a better guy than he is. Zelda wants to know what other guy. Thus she learns from Engstaad where she is really drifting, that she is beginning to love Carter without knowing it. She still thought she was in love with Tyler. She has never even thought of marrying Carter, though her own truthfulness and honesty force her to admit to Engstaad that she will marry him if he asks her.

She gets a message from Carter's aunt asking her to call on her. Zelda asks Engstaad to drive her out in his car. She is forewarned now. She tells the aunt she will marry Carter if he asks her. The aunt examines Zelda, sees her character: honesty, desire for decency, etc.; realizes that Zelda will make a good wife. But the aunt cannot overlook Zelda's background and family. But there is nothing against Zelda, no way in which she can break up the engagement. The meeting ends in stalemate.

While driving back with Engstaad, they pass the Middleton house. Zelda tells him that is the house she dreams about, etc. She tells him she intends to marry Carter. Engstaad wants to know what about the child, advises her not to tell Carter. Zelda says she will tell him first. Engstaad realizes that, being Zelda, she could do nothing else.

The second rape occurs. It is learned now that the attacker is not a Negro but a white man with his face blacked with shoe-polish.

Lathe asks Zelda for money. She refuses. Lathe says O.K., but maybe she will change her mind, intimates blackmail, that he knows something her rich friend Carter might be interested in or maybe even the newspapers. She begins to comprehend, goes to her room. The locked drawer has been rifled. The picture and letters are gone.

She meets Engstaad, tells him. She knows Lathe has them. She is not afraid of Lathe's telling Carter, though she would rather have told him herself. She is afraid of what Lathe's warped brain might decide to do with them, what scandal he might start; whereupon Carter's

aunt would have been right in her objections to the
marriage. She realizes the harm it might do Carter's
career in Savannah. Engstaad says he will get the papers
back, even if he has to take Lathe apart in the process;
he would rather like that anyway. Zelda tells him she will
handle that. Besides, Carter has not asked her yet.

Carter wins the Negro's case. He asks Zelda to marry
him. She promises him an answer tomorrow and returns to make a search of Lathe's room before he can
give the papers to a newspaper. She finds the shoe-
blacking. She knows that Lathe is the rapist.

The third rape, and the murder. Engstaad saves
Lathe from the mob and gets him safely to jail.

Zelda tells Carter about the child. He is shocked. But
he says he still wants to marry her. But she sees he has
cold feet now. She tells him he is free. He refuses to
accept his dismissal, insists on taking Lathe's case. She
warns him of what it will do to him in Savannah. He still
insists. The case is tried, the letters and picture and
Zelda's motherhood are made public during the trial.
Lathe is sentenced, commits suicide in jail. That is the
end for Carter, though he still insists on keeping his
word to marry Zelda. But she knows better. She goes to
see the aunt of her own accord, renounces Carter, ends
it by telling the aunt to tell him she is going away with
Engstaad.

Zelda and Engstaad leave Savannah. She asks to pass
the Middleton house. She is silently saying goodbye to it
and to the dream of her youth, too. Engstaad produces
a deed to it. He has bought it for her; they will move into
it and be damned to Savannah and all of them if she says
the word. She says no, never. They go on.

Zelda and Engstaad on train. He shows her a newspaper, notice of Carter's engagement to a girl of his class.

Zelda and Engstaad before a marriage clerk, rapid brisk and business-like ceremony, soon over.

New Orleans. Ten years later. Engstaad and Zelda are married. They live very respectably and quietly, though Engstaad is still of the underworld and is not quite rich. Zelda's son, Glynn, is now in a good eastern prep school, knows nothing about his origin nor even about his so-called father's business. Zelda is happy, living only for her son, to keep him from ever knowing about her past.

Engstaad becomes involved in a gangster feud, is shot and killed. When his affairs are settled, the biggest and most profitable item left is the house in Savannah. Zelda knew very little about his affairs. She discovers that the house in Savannah is a high-class exclusive and very profitable brothel.

Savannah. Seven years later. Zelda now lives the quiet and retired life of a well-to-do widow. Teppie manages the brothel, which still prospers. Nobody but Teppie knows that Zelda has any connection with it. Zelda is continuing the business for her son's sake, to complete his education and give him a decent start in life; he is to fulfill the dream for which she has long ago given up any hope herself. Glynn has never even visited Savannah. She arranges each year for them to spend his vacation somewhere else; he is never to know how his mother lives. But he will graduate this spring, and Zelda realizes for the first time that he is almost a man now, and she cannot hope to hide the business from him much longer. The time has come for her to get out of it.

She is arranging with Teppie to end it before Glynn comes home.

Carter is married to the woman of whom his aunt approved. They are childless; his wife did not want the bother and inconvenience of children. She has become an extravagant, idle, dissatisfied shrew, dissatisfied with Carter's income and his lack of ambition for money, his radical social ideas which Zelda taught him. Carter, as an escape from his home life, is engaged in civic work, not in local politics but involved with them in a struggle for cleaner government. He is not a bigot, but merely opposed to corruption and such. He is now on a citizens' committee. The item with which they are occupied is the quietly notorious brothel which Zelda owns. The brothel itself is not the question so much, but the fact that it has no police record and has never caused any scandal indicates that its owner is someone high in city government, and the committee wishes to know who this is as a means of undermining the group which controls the city. The committee is divided into two groups: one headed by Carter, reasonable, well-meaning, temperate; the other headed by Parmalee, a wealthy religious fanatic and moralist who believes himself to be the appointed scourge of the Lord. The two groups are already antagonistic. Parmalee, using a hired spy, an unsavory man to whom Carter has already taken a violent antipathy, has discovered by bribery and betrayal of a servant where Zelda lives and under what name. Parmalee wants to raid her with police, run her in and give her the third degree like any streetwalker taken in the act. Carter and his group object, not only because she is a woman but because of the method by which they gained the information as well as the instrument they used: the spy, bragging of his own lowness, saying how Zelda herself looked pretty good, he could go for her, etc. Parmalee accuses Dan of protecting vice. Carter says he objects only to the means used. By a majority vote, Carter is permitted to go and see the woman first before any further steps are taken. Dan returns to his office, has an investigation made, discovers quickly that the spy has a criminal record and has a sentence hanging over him.

He calls on the woman. It is Zelda. He cannot believe it. She assures him it is so, tells him why—it is for her son. Dan is severe, bitter, distant. He still loves her, thinks he conceals it. At last he agrees to give her time to close the place decently, for the sake of the girls as well as to shield her son from any public scandal, notoriety.

Dan reports to his committee. He and Parmalee almost come to blows. Parmalee accuses him of being in the pay of vice and corruption, or even of shielding the woman and the house for his own immoral purposes. He snatches telephone, calls police and demands a raiding party with a warrant; he will have a man ready to go along and identify the woman. Dan goes to his office, calls Zelda and warns her to leave the apartment and not go near the brothel as it will be watched too, asks her to get in touch with him when she is settled safely somewhere. He then intercepts the spy and tells him if he does not leave town at once, he will turn him over to the police on the old charge. The spy tries to brazen it out, then cringes and whines, promises to leave town. The game is up with him now, but he will get what revenge he can. He writes an anonymous letter to Carter's wife, then hurriedly and furtively hunts up a reporter he knows.

The police arrive at the committee rooms, but the spy can't be found. Parmalee orders them to raid Zelda's apartment anyhow. She is gone. The maid does not know where; they get no information from her. Parmalee sets his hired detectives to watch the brothel in case Zelda appears there.

The reporter calls on Parmalee, to know whether to break the story or not. He tells Parmalee the spy told him that the woman has a son, Glynn Engstaad, in an eastern prep school. Parmalee tells the reporter to wait, and sends for Dan. He threatens Dan with what the reporter can print unless Dan behaves. Dan says print and be damned, exits. Parmalee thinks a moment, rings for a secretary and dictates a telegram to Glynn: "Mother dangerously ill. Come home at once. Dr. Montgomery," and dismisses secretary. He tells the reporter to hold the story, it will be a lot bigger in a day or two.

The reporter goes to Carter. He says he has already given the dope to Parmalee and he will play ball with Dan, too. He tells Dan about the telegram Parmalee sent. They both realize the import: that Parmalee knows that Glynn will find his mother somehow and they have only to trail Glynn. Dan asks the reporter to hold the story until it does become public news. The reporter agrees. No message has come from Zelda. Dan tries to find her, but fails. The maid either knows nothing, or is afraid, and he does not dare call the brothel because he has found that Parmalee's men are watching him, too. He telephones a friend in New York and asks to have

Glynn shadowed to the train and himself notified what train.

Dan's wife has received the spy's letter. She makes a scene with Dan. She tells him she doesn't care how many whores he has, but she will not have her name and herself as his wife dragged through the mud, too. She delivers an ultimatum to him to drop the whole thing, or else. Dan is gentle still, tries to explain. She won't listen; she has warned him.

The reporter calls on Teppie at the brothel. He is a little tight. He tells Teppie the developments so far, a good story, but he is holding it off by request for a while. But he doesn't like it. He is just a lousy newspaper bloke, but there is something about it which stinks even to him: Parmalee is a bigotted old so-and-so and Dan is a good guy even though he is a sissy. He tells Teppie about the wire Parmalee sent to Glynn. Teppie telephones Zelda at her hiding place. Zelda orders Teppie to start clearing the house at once. She calls Glynn's school, but he has already left.

Dan gets a wire from his friend in New York saying what train Glynn is on. Dan has not yet found Zelda. His only hope now is to meet Glynn at the train and keep him from leading Parmalee's men to Zelda's hiding place. He will know Glynn, he is convinced; any man will recognize the child of the only woman he ever loved, no matter who fathered it.

Glynn and Parmalee's son on a train bound for Savannah. Glynn is seventeen, distracted over his mother's illness. Parmalee is twenty-one or -two, tight and getting tighter. He crashes in on Glynn; they are bound for the same place, it seems. Parmalee is a junior at college, is slipping off to spend the weekend with his girl in the swellest brothel in the U.S., most exclusive, owned by a society woman, though nobody knows it. Glynn is restive under this drunken harangue, is worried about his mother; the train seems to crawl. Nevertheless, he has to listen, getting a picture of the brothel but without associating it with anything and not even conscious that he is remembering details. Parmalee is slipping into town without his father's knowledge; if his old man knew he was cutting school it would be bad enough, but to know where he was really bound, how he was going to spend the weekend; his father is an old mossback puritan, etc., etc. He tells Glynn how he keeps a car at the first stop outside Savannah and gets off there and not only slips into town unseen but beats the train in. He offers to take Glynn with him in the car. Frantic over his mother, Glynn accepts to get there quicker.

Dan and Zelda waiting at the station. They do not see one another.

Glynn and Parmalee racing toward Savannah in the car. They enter the town, pass the brothel. Parmalee points it out to Glynn, extols its parts again. Glynn, near home now, pays less attention than ever. He remembers the house unconsciously, not aware that he has done so.

Glynn reaches his mother's address and interviews the frightened maid who has never seen him before. Two of Parmalee's men are waiting to trail him. The maid does not know where his mother is, disclaims all knowledge of the illness. Glynn is now frantic, tells the maid Zelda is his mother, demands her whereabouts. The maid gives him the street and number of the brothel. Glynn hurries away, the detectives following him. The maid calls Teppie at the brothel, tells her what has happened.

Dan and Zelda at the station. They have not seen one another. The train comes in. Glynn is not on it. As Zelda turns away, she is paged to the telephone. It is Teppie, who tells her Glynn was at the apartment and is headed now for the brothel, breaks off: "Here he comes now—" Zelda hurries out for a taxi. Dan sees her, too late. He follows in another one.

The brothel. Parmalee, Junior, and Teppie. Parmalee is quite drunk now. He is demanding his girl, any girl. He looks about, sees signs of hurried vacating. Teppie can't handle him, backs slowly away before him as he follows her up the stairs.

Zelda, then a moment later, Dan, enters the brothel. Parmalee's men recognize Dan. One telephones Parmalee, is ordered to watch and wait.

Glynn reaches the brothel. He recognizes it now. He doesn't understand; he cannot believe his senses. Yet the number is the right one which the maid gave him, and his mother is ill. He hurries in. Parmalee's spy informs Parmalee over the wire. Parmalee orders them to go on in; they have the warrant.

The brothel. Glynn enters. He, too, sees the hurried signs; he recognizes as though by instinct what the place really is. The address must be wrong. Then he hears the voices from upstairs, and recognizes his mother's. He hurries up the stairs. Zelda is facing Parmalee, Junior, drunk, loud, demanding girls. As Glynn enters, Parmalee says Zelda will do then, not so bad for an old bat at that, approaches and attempts the attack. Glynn leaps upon him. Teppie snaps off the lights. Sound of a fall. Zelda's voice: "Turn on the lights, Teppie." Parmalee's men begin to hammer at the front door. The lights go on. Parmalee, Junior, is lying at the foot of the stairs, dead, Zelda bending over him, her dress torn. Glynn stands dazed, amazed with grief and despair while Dan grasps his arm. Zelda tells Teppie to go and open the door. Teppie exits. Zelda is examining something in Parmalee's hand. It is a button torn from Glynn's coat. She rises and asks Glynn for his coat, to cover her torn dress. He removes the coat, dazed, hands it to her, shrinking, waking now in grief and horror. She puts on the coat as Parmalee's men enter. Leader: "We don't want that punk. Let him go. Here's the two we want."

A DISSOLVE of newspaper headlines: Vice ring broken. Prominent lawyer captured in raid following underworld murder. Wife sues for divorce, etc.

Zelda in a jail cell. She is anxious, hoping against hope that Glynn will come to speak to her, knowing that he will not. A policewoman enters, tells her with gruff sympathy that no message has come yet; give the boy a little time: false reassurance which they both know Zelda sees through. Zelda keeps her head up.

The arraignment. Old Parmalee presses the business. He is grieving for his son but pretends otherwise, believes he does not grieve, refusing sympathy: sin has been punished, the wages of it are death, let who must suffer. As for himself, he doesn't even suffer: that son was no son of his, etc. Dan tries to assume the blame. Zelda explodes his story, proves by the button clutched in Parmalee's hand that she pushed him down the stairs. The court delivers its opinion harshly: that the torn dress constituted an attempt at assault and Zelda is freed, but must leave Savannah forever.

The cell. The policewoman brings Zelda a note from Glynn. She opens it eagerly, believing despite herself. It says goodbye, he cannot see her again. Dan enters with the key, unlocks the cell himself, leads her out, explains that he has been constituted to conduct her out of Savannah, some end-line such as farther than that, until they die, etc. They walk down the corridor and out of the jail together.

FADE OUT.

THE END